IS CAROLE PLAYING SECOND FIDDLE?

"We won again!" crowed Stevie, bouncing up and down.

Lisa playfully punched a flushed Zach in the arm. "You rock!"

"Zach, that was fantastic," Carole admitted. Actually she was a little concerned about the possible injury to Barq's ankles from the sliding stop, but she didn't want to belittle the boy's amazing performance. After all, if it hadn't been for him, they wouldn't have won.

I doubt Barq knew what was coming, Carole thought, but before she could respond, the other riders rushed up to congratulate Zach. She found herself bumped out of the way by his crowd of newfound admirers.

the SADDLE CLUB

NEW RIDER

BONNIE BRYANT

A SKYLARK BOOK
NEW YORK • TORONTO • LONDON • SYDNEY • AUCKLAND

Special thanks to Sir "B" Farms
and Laura Roper

RL: 5, ages 009–012

NEW RIDER
A Bantam Skylark Book / January 2001

ISBN 0-553-48700-0

Visit us on the Web! www.randomhouse.com/kids
Educators and librarians, for a variety of teaching tools, visit us at
www.randomhouse.com/teachers

Published simultaneously in the United States and Canada

Bantam Skylark is an imprint of Random House Children's Books, a division of
Random House, Inc. SKYLARK BOOK and colophon and BANTAM
BOOKS and colophon are registered trademarks of Random House, Inc.
Bantam Books, 1540 Broadway, New York, New York 10036.

PRINTED IN THE UNITED STATES OF AMERICA
OPM   10 9 8 7 6 5 4 3 2 1

*My special thanks
to Cat Johnston for her
help in the writing of
this book.*

*And thanks also to
Dr. Michael Thompson
for his wisdom
and inspiration.*

AS STEVIE LAKE hurried across the yard of Pine Hollow Stables, late as usual, it was all she could do to keep from breaking into a run. She spied her two best friends, Lisa Atwood and Carole Hanson, standing next to a horse trailer and jogged over to join them.

"Did I miss anything?" she called anxiously.

Carole gave her a disapproving look. "I can't believe you could be late on a day like today."

Lisa chuckled. "Remember, this is Stevie you're talking about."

Carole smiled ruefully. "You're right. I don't know what I was thinking."

"It's not my fault," Stevie insisted.

Lisa slipped an arm around her friend's shoulders. "Never is, never will be."

"Oh come on, guys, give me a break. You know what Saturday mornings are like at my house."

"Brothers?" Lisa asked sympathetically.

Stevie grimaced. "Lisa, you should wash your mouth out with soap for using that word." She had three brothers, one younger, one older, and a twin. As much as she loved them, there were times she felt they had been put on the planet for the sole purpose of her personal torture. Of course, she was not about to admit that her own love of practical jokes sometimes justified their actions.

Stevie was the practical joker and the most high-spirited of the three friends. But right now she wasn't thinking about revenge on her brothers. Instead she craned her neck, trying to see into the trailer. "Have they even unloaded her yet?"

"Not yet," Carole answered, almost in a whisper.

"It seems Sunset is being a little shy about viewing her new home," Lisa told Stevie. "And, of course, Mr. Wooten has to be extra careful."

There came the sound of scuffling from inside the vehicle.

"You'd be surprised how many horses are injured getting out of a trailer," Carole said, watching anxiously. "The extra weight on their ankles from backing down a ramp can cause a sprain or stress fracture, not to mention the possibility of falling off the edge." She shuddered at the thought. "If that's not enough, there's the added danger of rupturing the uterine artery during transportation of a mare as pregnant as this one."

Of the three girls, Carole was the most knowledgeable about horses. She had made up her mind that whatever she did with the rest of her life, it was going to involve these wonderful animals. She was seriously considering becoming a veterinarian, so she had spent a lot of time making rounds with Judy Barker, the local equine vet.

"Look, I think Max is coming to the rescue," Stevie said.

The owner of Pine Hollow, Maximilian Regnery III—whom everybody called Max—strode up the loading ramp and disappeared into the trailer. He was an expert horseman, as well as the instructor for the girls' Pony Club, Horse Wise. Right now he was supervising the arrival of the new mare.

"If anyone can coax her out, it's Max," Lisa said with certainty.

Sure enough, a few moments later the girls saw the rump of the animal as the mare backed cautiously but steadily down the ramp. When she reached the ground, she threw her head up and snorted as though she'd been offended.

"If it's so dangerous to move a pregnant mare, why don't they let her give birth at her home stable and *then* bring her here?" Lisa asked. Although she was a year older than Carole and Stevie, Lisa was the newest to the sport of riding. She had natural talent but wasn't yet as knowledgeable about the animals as her two friends were.

The three friends loved spending their time learning about horses almost as much as they loved riding and being with horses. In fact, together the three girls had formed The Saddle Club. It was a club with only two rules: First, you had to be head over heels in love with horses, and second, you had to be willing to help the other members out, no matter what.

"That's a good question, Lisa."

The girls turned to find Judy Barker standing behind them.

"Mr. Wooten wants to get as many foals out of Sunset as he can before she gets too old, and the next best time for getting her pregnant will be immediately after she gives birth, because mares go into heat about a week after they foal. Also, it's a lot less dangerous to move her now than it would be to transport a nervous mother and a fragile newborn."

The horse was covered with a light blanket to keep her warm during travel, so the girls couldn't see her conformation. They waited expectantly as Mr. Wooten stripped the cover off.

"What a looker!" Stevie exclaimed.

"She obviously has excellent bloodlines," Carole observed.

"You're right, Carole," Max said, striding toward the group. "Sunset's a very valuable broodmare, and many of her offspring have been quite successful. Let's hope Geronimo can add quality." Geronimo was Pine Hollow's stallion. Mr. Wooten was paying to breed Sunset with him.

Lisa was puzzled by Max's last remark. "If she's as valuable as you say, what makes you think she doesn't have quality?"

Max smiled at her. "*Adding quality* is a horse breeders' term for a stallion's ability to pass on his best traits to his offspring. It doesn't mean Sunset's aren't good, but we hope to make them even better in her next foal." He turned to Judy. "Would you like to look her over now?"

"Absolutely," said the vet, moving toward the animal.

"In the meantime I'd like the three of you to double-check the foaling stall for me. We want to make sure our new tenant is absolutely comfortable and safe, right?"

"You got it, Max," Carole said, throwing him a playful salute. They headed inside the stable.

"I wish they wouldn't put the foaling stalls so far from the regular ones," Lisa said. "It's going to make it harder to keep an eye on Sunset."

"They have to," Stevie replied, grabbing a handful of hay and banking it a little steeper against the foaling stall's rounded corners. "Horses are pretty nosy creatures, so all the ones that don't have babies will want to meet the new one. That might upset the dam."

"There's also a small chance that the foal might get confused and think a different animal was its mother," Carole offered as she checked the water supply and manger. "It's called imprinting. Foals need to imprint on the right mother."

A few moments later, Max and Judy arrived leading Sunset. On either side of them, curious horses peered out from their stalls, watching the newcomer. Max and Judy took her into the stall and stayed with her to make sure nothing in the unfamiliar surroundings alarmed her.

To Stevie, Sunset appeared completely indifferent

to both Max *and* her new surroundings. Instead she seemed more interested in going outside to her private little paddock.

"What do you say, Judy? Is it okay to let her go?" Max asked.

"She's fit and healthy, Max. I don't think you'll have any excitement around here for at least three weeks."

"Oh, I don't know about that," he said, unclipping Sunset's halter and allowing her to move outside. "Unless I'm mistaken, there's a mounted Horse Wise meeting in a few minutes." He looked pointedly at Lisa, Stevie, and Carole. "Not to mention that we have a new member starting today. Don't you girls have some getting ready to do?"

"In all the excitement I almost forgot," admitted Carole.

"We'd better get moving," Stevie urged.

Lisa hurried after her friends "Hey, do you two know who this new rider is?"

"I haven't got a clue," Stevie said as she entered the locker room.

"Why should today be any different?" said a haughty voice from the corner. Veronica diAngelo was putting on lip gloss.

Stevie glared at her. "Oh, terrific, it's Pine Hollow's answer to the Wicked Witch of the West. Exactly what I need."

"I'd say what you need is someone to dress you in the morning," Veronica smirked. "Nice shirt, Lake. Hah!" She strode out the door.

Veronica diAngelo was a thorn in the side of The Saddle Club. She was rich, and she never let anyone forget it. She was also spoiled and lazy, and she tried to get everyone else to do her work. She and Stevie especially seemed to rub each other the wrong way.

Stevie looked down at her shirt. Okay, it was a little wrinkled, but outside of that what was wrong with it? She was about to go after Veronica and give her a few choice words, but Carole blocked her path.

"Let it go, the meeting's going to start in a minute."

"I know who it is," Lisa suddenly volunteered.

"Who what is?" Stevie asked, confused by Lisa's abrupt change of subject.

"I know who the new rider is," Lisa insisted.

"Who?" cried Carole.

"How long have you known?" demanded Stevie.

"Who?" repeated Carole.

8

Lisa laughed. "You sound like an owl."

"Who, who, who?" Carole said, playing along.

"Zach," Lisa declared triumphantly.

"The new boy from school?" squealed Carole.

"You got it in one," Lisa confirmed.

"Excuse me," said Stevie.

"I didn't know he was into horses," Carole said.

"Excuse me," Stevie said louder. "I seem to have had a flat tire on the information highway."

"Sorry, Stevie. I forgot you don't go to our school. Zachary Simpson just moved here, but I'm not sure from where."

"He's kind of cute, too," added Carole.

"Cute and into horses . . . ," Stevie speculated. "Sounds promising."

"Hey, you're booked, remember!" Lisa reminded her.

"Booked, yes. Embalmed, no," Stevie declared with a grin.

"What does Phil think about this liberal attitude?" asked Carole, crossing her arms.

"Just kidding." Stevie looked anxiously from friend to friend. "You do know I'm kidding, right?"

Phil Marsten was Stevie's steady boyfriend. Because he lived about twenty minutes from Willow Creek, they didn't get to see each other very often, but they called each other almost every day and got together whenever they could.

Lisa laughed. "Don't worry. We know you're devoted to Phil."

"Come on, you two, we've got to scoot or we'll be late for the meeting."

THE SADDLE CLUB girls were among the last to enter the room. Stevie spotted the new rider immediately. He was lounging against a wall. Tall and slender, his hair was almost white-blond, and long bangs hung over his eyes. His shirt sleeves were rolled back, and Stevie could tell by his muscles that he exercised. "Hey, Carole," she whispered. "You were right, he is kind of cute."

"Okay, everyone, settle down," Max called. "We have a busy day ahead of us. As you all know, today I've planned a gymkhana."

A buzz of excitement swept the room. Everybody loved games on horseback.

"In a few minutes I'm going to divide you up into teams, but first I'd like to introduce you to the newest member of our Horse Wise group, Zachary Simpson." He gestured to the boy. "I know you'll all do your best to make him feel welcome. Zachary, would you like to say a few words?"

10

Stevie thought the boy looked a bit self-conscious as he moved toward Max. He pushed his bangs to the side and gave a shy grin.

"Well, first of all, you can call me Zach. My family just moved here from California." He slipped his hands in his pockets as if he didn't know what to do with them. "I'm new to all this horse stuff. I mean *really* new. I went to stay with my cousin in Texas for a while and he took me riding, which turned out to be pretty awesome, so I decided it would be cool to learn more about it." He shrugged. "I guess that's why I'm here."

"I'd like to think you came to the right place, Zach," Max said. "That's what Pine Hollow is all about. Learning."

There were murmurs of agreement throughout the room.

"I've posted a list outside showing who's on which team for the gymkhana. Everyone tack up and meet me in the outdoor ring. Pronto."

"Come on, you two, I'll introduce you to Zach," Lisa offered.

Carole agreed. "Yeah, like Max said, we should make him feel welcome. Maybe show him the ropes."

The girls trooped outside to find Zach waiting his turn to see the list.

Lisa joined him. "Hi, Zach. I'm Lisa. We're both in Mrs. Mathios's social studies class.

"Sure, I remember," he responded with a smile.

"These are my friends, Carole and Stevie. They're the best riders at Pine Hollow."

"That's a matter of opinion," Veronica diAngelo snorted.

"That's Veronica," Stevie said. "Feel free to ignore her. Everybody else does."

"Do you know which horse Max assigned you?" Lisa asked.

"Yeah, his name is Barq. I got to see him when Max gave me the grand tour."

Stevie was surprised. "I guess Max has confidence in your riding abilities then. Barq is pretty spirited."

"I like that in a horse," Zach assured her.

"Hey, guys," Carole called. "I checked the list and guess what? We're all on the same team!"

"You mean all three of us?" asked Stevie excitedly.

"Nope." Carole shook her head. "All four!"

"I'm on your team?" Zach asked.

"That definitely puts you guys out of the running," crowed Veronica. "With a beginner on your team, I suggest you don't even bother to play." With a laugh, she flounced away.

Stevie bristled. "I've got a few suggestions I'd like to share with her, too!"

"She's probably right," Zach said. "I may tank the whole thing for you."

"Look, you do your best," Carole told him. "That's all we want."

"Come on. We'll help you tack up," Lisa offered.

WHEN CAROLE WAS finished saddling Starlight, she went to talk to Stevie. "What did you think of Zach's saddling technique?" she asked, careful to keep her voice low.

"He's kind of rough around the edges," Stevie chuckled. "But you can't fault him on his enthusiasm."

Carole rested her chin on her arms as she leaned on the stall door. "That's true, but we could have given him a lot more pointers if he hadn't been so impatient to get in the saddle."

Stevie put the finishing touches to Belle and stroked her horse's long nose thoughtfully. "Maybe his blood was up. I know some days all I want to do is hit the trail and not bother with all the other stuff."

"I know how that feels," Carole admitted, "but the

difference is that we *do* the other stuff no matter how eager we are to get going."

Stevie shrugged. "I wouldn't worry about it yet. I'm sure he'll settle down. We did." She led her horse out of the stall. "Now, let's go see how he rides."

As THE GIRLS guided their horses toward the stable exit, Zach, leading Barq, fell into step with them.

"Looks like Barq is raring to go," Lisa remarked, observing the prancing horse.

"That makes two of us," Zach said, smiling with undisguised enthusiasm.

Out of habit Carole found herself scanning his mount for any problems. One became immediately apparent. "Zach, you know you're going to have to tighten up Barq's girth again before you mount, right?"

"I already did that when I tacked him up."

The group came to a halt.

"Barq is trying to pull a fast one on you," Lisa told him. She gestured toward the horse's belly.

15

Zach was clearly puzzled. "Looks okay to me."

Stevie stepped forward. "Here, I'll hold Barq while you give the girth a tug."

Zach did as she suggested, and the leather slid a few inches tighter. "Hey! I know I pulled this as tight as I could the first time."

The girls all chuckled.

"Barq took a big breath of air and held it just as you pulled, then he let it out when you were done," Lisa told him. "It's an old horse trick. A lot of animals do it, so it's something you have to check for every time you saddle up."

"Otherwise when you put your weight in the stirrup to mount, you'll find yourself sitting on the ground and your saddle under his belly," Carole warned him.

"If you pull it as tight as you can, then walk him around for a minute, he'll have to exhale. When you hear him do that, you quickly make it tighter," Stevie added.

"I didn't think horses were that smart," Zach said.

Carole shared a knowing look with her friends. "Boy, are you in for some surprises!"

Sunset poked her head over her door to see what was going on.

"Hey, girl." Zach reached out to stroke her. "Why the long face?"

16

Stevie immediately broke into laughter. "Why the long face! That's funny."

"Oh, I get it," Carole said after a moment and chuckled.

"Of course! All horses have long faces," Lisa giggled, catching on.

Sunset avoided Zach's touch by moving deeper into her stall.

"Not very friendly, is she?" he remarked. "And, wow, does someone need to go on a diet, big time!"

Carole rushed to the mare's defense. "She's not fat, Zach. She's pregnant."

Zach made a face. "Pregnant and a half from the look of her."

"For your information, she's due to give birth sometime in the next three weeks," Carole told him. "Then they'll breed her with Geronimo. I really want to be here for the birth!"

"Me too," agreed Stevie.

"Me three!" Lisa cried.

"Well, count me out," Zach said.

The girls all looked at each other with astonishment. Why would anyone pass up the chance to see a foal born?

"Maybe if you knew a little more about it, you wouldn't feel uncomfortable," Carole suggested.

Zach held up a hand. "I took biology. I know the drill."

"Then you know it's a perfectly natural process," Lisa said.

"So is vomiting," he pointed out. "That doesn't mean I want to watch it happen. Besides, all I want to do is ride."

Carole could hardly believe her ears. "There's a lot more to riding than just"—she foundered for a moment—"riding."

Stevie looked at Lisa and rolled her eyes. They knew what was coming next; they'd heard it before. Carole was about to launch into her "Horse Care as a Critical Piece of the Riding Experience" talk. A lecture guaranteed to frighten away any new rider. Something had to be done, and quick.

"When you ride these animals you take on certain obligations," Carole started, oblivious to her friends' imploring looks. "They're trusting you with their health, their very lives. In return for that, you assume certain responsibilities. In order to know when your horse is sick, it's important to know how it looks and behaves when it's well. They rely on you for food and shelter, so you have to know how and when and what to feed them—What the . . . ?" She was startled out of her passionate speech by the feel of Stevie's finger pok-

18

ing in her ear. "What are you doing?" she cried, swatting the hand away.

"You seemed to be having a brain hemorrhage," Stevie said. "I was applying direct pressure."

Zach burst out laughing.

Carole glared at Stevie. She had been about to impart some very important information to a new rider, and she didn't think it was nice of her to interrupt.

"Hey, C," Zach said to Carole, "you really had me. For a minute there I was about to run screaming from the stable and never get in the saddle again. I know riding means responsibility, but right now I just want to ride."

Carole suddenly realized what Stevie had been trying to tell her. She had almost driven Zach away by loading him up with too much information too fast and too soon. "Oh, well . . . ha ha," she chuckled weakly. "Gotcha."

Lisa smacked her lightly on the back. "Yep, our Carole is quite the kidder."

"Don't you think we should get going?" asked Zach, looking longingly toward the exit. "I don't want to miss anything." Without waiting, he started for the stable door.

Lisa hurried after him. "Zach, don't forget to touch the horseshoe before you mount up!"

He paused, waiting for her. "Why would I do that?"

"It's tradition. No rider who touches it has ever been seriously hurt."

As Lisa and Zach left the stable, Stevie cornered Carole. "What were you *thinking*?"

"Guess I got carried away," Carole admitted sheepishly.

Stevie shrugged and smiled. "You had good intentions, anyway."

"I hear the road to Hades is paved with those," Carole replied.

"And that it leads directly to Veronica diAngelo's house," quipped Stevie.

They both laughed and followed the others outside.

STEVIE ON BELLE and Carole on Starlight drew up next to Lisa and Zach in the outdoor ring. Max cleared his throat and everyone immediately fell silent. "As many of you know, the original purpose for gymkhana was to perfect a rider's skill with mounted weapons and to train horses in combat tactics and absolute obedience. Of course, in modern times we've changed that a bit. Skill and obedience are still the main focus, but now fun and good sportsmanship are also encouraged. Hopefully you will all have a chance to experience that today."

"What? No more battle-axes?" Zach whispered with a smile.

"Sorry, Veronica's the only one we have left," Stevie mumbled back.

Max drew their attention to the ring. "I've set up a barrel race for our first competition. Each team has four members, but only the top three scores will count. The fastest combined times will win the event. You have two minutes to decide who rides in what position for your team. Good luck."

"Have you ever ridden in a barrel race before?" Lisa asked Zach as Max walked away.

"Not barrels, no," he admitted. "But we did something similar when I was in Texas, and I have seen it at a rodeo."

"Here's what I suggest," Carole said, taking charge. "Stevie will lead off, which should get us off to a good start. Lisa, you go next, then me, and then Zach." She turned to the boy. "That way with three good scores in already, you won't be under any pressure."

Zach smiled and gave her a thumbs-up. "Whatever you guys decide is fine by me. After all, I am the amateur here."

"Rank amateur," gloated Veronica diAngelo from the group next to them. "We're going to wipe you guys off the map."

"Ignore her and focus on what we have to do," Lisa advised.

They all nodded agreement.

Stevie, who was first out for their team, didn't let them down. From the minute she left the starting line, her ride was smooth as silk. She and Belle negotiated each turn cleanly and sailed home at a gallop with a fine time.

Lisa was next. Knowing her friend tended to get nervous about competition, Carole had made sure to give her a reassuring word before she took off. There was no way to be sure if that's what did the trick, but Lisa and Prancer also turned in a more-than-respectable time.

Carole felt her pulse begin to race with excitement as she prepared herself for her turn. Although they already had two good scores, Veronica diAngelo's team was also doing well. As much as she liked Zach, she had to be realistic. This was his first try, and they couldn't count on him. It was up to her to cement their victory.

Starlight broke from the line fast and straight, Carole thrilling to the power of the horse beneath her. They rounded the first barrel at a good clip and aimed for the second one. *Whoosh!* They took that one even closer and faster. With the blood singing in her ears, she took aim at the last one. Anticipating the turn of Starlight's body around the barrel, Carole leaned in as she had been taught. Unfortunately, at that moment she felt her horse stumble and almost go down. Although Starlight managed to catch himself, her foot struck the barrel with enough force to knock it over. They were disqualified!

Carole guided her horse back to the finish line, flushing with embarrassment.

Her teammates hurried over to console her.

"Sorry, guys," she mumbled. "Guess I blew it."

"That was a bad break, that's all," Stevie said sympathetically.

Lisa put a consoling hand on her shoulder. "I really thought you had it for a minute."

Zach, on the other hand, seemed all revved up. "You were totally smoking, C!" he raved.

Carole was taken aback. Didn't he realize because of her mistake they had lost the competition?

"That was an excellent try. I can't wait for my turn."

Carole was about to give him some advice about how to negotiate the turns when she thought better of it. After all, she had blown it completely. "Guess you're about to get your chance. I'm sure you'll do fine." She gave a rueful grin. "You can't do worse than I did."

Zach gave them a thumbs-up and maneuvered Barq to the starting line, where the restless animal pranced and fretted. His rider seemed to barely have him under control.

The starting bell rang.

Zach and Barq left the line almost in sync with the sound, and from there on out it was all flying elbows, flapping knees, and galloping horse. The duo flew around the barrels, Barq's flashing hooves sending showers of dirt into the air as they negotiated the turns at hair-raising speed.

Carole was certain they would knock over at least one barrel, if not all of them. How could they not, with that out-of-control style? She continued to watch in amazement. Not only did the barrels stay up, but the dynamic duo flashed across the finish line with the best time of the meet!

The Saddle Club rushed over to Zach as he and Barq skidded to a stop. Zach's legs were way out of position and he almost came out of the saddle, but he managed to hang on with the help of a handful of mane.

"Yahoo!" Stevie shouted.

"That was amazing!" Lisa raved.

"Why didn't you tell us you could do that?" Carole asked.

Zach shrugged modestly. "I told you I've never been in a barrel race before, but my cousin taught me to do the same thing around cactus back in Texas."

"Guess you'd think twice before knocking over one of those," Lisa laughed.

"Especially if you know what's good for your horse," Carole mumbled to herself.

Max called the class together. "I am pleased to announce the winner of the barrel racing competition . . . Group Three."

Carole felt her heart leap. They had done it! They had beaten Veronica and her team! She turned to the others and her spirits dropped a bit. Lisa, Stevie, and Zach were already celebrating their victory. In all fairness, she had to admit that she hadn't been of any help.

"One more announcement before we set up for the next event," continued Max. "Zach Simpson has set the fastest barrel racing time of any Horse Wise member ever."

All the riders went over to congratulate him.

"Nice job, Zach," Carole called over the mob. In her mind she was thinking, *Beginner's luck*.

The next event was a flag relay race. Unlike the first game, all the teams would compete at the same time. At the bell the riders would run to their horses, mount, gallop as fast as they could to the other end of the arena, snatch a red flag out of a cone on the ground, return to the starting point, dismount, and tag the next member, who could then begin.

The Saddle Club team agreed to keep the same order as before.

At the start of the race, Stevie dashed over to Belle and mounted her in one fluid, graceful motion. It set the tone for the rest of her round—fast, smooth, and elegant, resulting in a small lead for their team.

As Stevie slapped Lisa's hand, the other girl yelled, "Thanks!" grateful for the head start.

Because she had been so instrumental in Lisa's training, Carole watched her compete with all the pleasure of a mother duck watching her beloved duckling excel at swimming—proud of the way Prancer's and Lisa's movements were so coordinated. The trust between horse and rider was rewarded, and they managed to hang on to the lead Stevie and Belle had gained.

Carole gathered herself for her chance, determined to do better this time. The moment Lisa slipped off Prancer's back and high-fived her, she raced to Starlight's side, who stood stock-still as she had taught him to do. Then, at her urging, Starlight took off like a shot. Not wanting to overrun the flags, Carole reined her horse in slightly and managed to grab one. Again she cued her horse into a fast gallop, heading back to the starting point. Pulling to a halt, Carole slid smoothly out of the saddle and promptly tripped over her own feet. To her horror she felt the flag fly from her hand as she landed on her hands and knees. Arena dust filled her eyes, temporarily blinding her. Desperately she felt around on the ground for it.

"To your right!" Stevie yelled. "It's on your right, Carole!"

She felt her fingers close around the cloth and, stomach churning and eyes watering, managed to stumble to the finish line where Zach was waiting for his turn.

"Sorry," she gasped as they touched hands.

Zach said nothing. He was already on his way to the prancing Barq.

"Oh no!" Lisa cried. "Barq's overexcited. Zach will never be able to mount him!"

Once again they had underestimated their teammate. Instead of approaching his horse from the left, Zach ran straight at Barq's rump. With a cry of "*Yeehaw!*" he leaped into the air and, using the animal's hindquarters as a vault, landed spectacularly in the saddle.

Carole's gasp of astonishment was echoed by everyone.

Without even securing his feet in the stirrups, Zach kicked Barq to a mad gallop and the horse responded for all it was worth. In a flash he managed to make up all the distance that Carole's fall had cost them. Traveling at what Carole felt was a foolhardy speed, he leaned down to grab a flag, then shot forward to pull even with Veronica, who was in the lead. It was a race to the finish! The two of them reached the starting point at the same time, but while Veronica dismounted the traditional way, Zach reined Barq to a screeching halt and propelled himself from the saddle, hitting the ground running and crossing the finish line before Veronica's expensive boots even touched the ground.

The three girls nearly turned themselves inside out with joy.

"We won again!" crowed Stevie, bouncing up and down.

Lisa playfully punched a flushed Zach in the arm. "You rock!"

"Zach, that was fantastic," Carole admitted. Actually she was a little concerned about the possible injury to Barq's ankles from the sliding stop, but she didn't want to belittle the boy's amazing performance. After all, if it hadn't been for him, they wouldn't have won.

"Where did you learn to mount a horse like that?" Stevie gasped.

Zach shrugged. "That's how all the cool kids did it in Texas, so I did, too."

"You have *got* to teach me that," Stevie insisted. "It is *so hot*."

"A little unnerving for the horse," Carole ventured.

"Not if you've prepared him," Stevie countered.

I doubt Barq knew what was coming, Carole thought, but before she could respond, the other riders rushed up to congratulate Zach. She found herself bumped out of the way by his crowd of newfound admirers.

Veronica diAngelo wormed her way to the center of the throng. "It looks like we have a virtuoso on our hands," she purred. "Maybe I misjudged you, Zachary."

"Don't worry, Veronica, I'll make sure he doesn't do the same to you," Stevie told her with a grin.

The last event of the afternoon was a paper chase. This event was a test of a rider's seat and the smoothness of a horse's gaits. After removing their saddles, the riders were to sit on a piece of paper. With Max calling out changes in gaits and directions, the one who could keep the paper in place the longest would get the most points.

Everybody was fine at the walk, but as soon as Max

called for a trot, many of the younger, inexperienced riders started to drop out. Unfortunately for The Saddle Club, Zach was among the first dismissed, due to his undisciplined seat and his difficulty controlling a now overexcited Barq.

He was clearly disappointed and Carole made a mental note to offer to work with him on his skills. Meanwhile she concentrated on her own performance, determined to win this event.

As it turned out, she did just that, even beating Stevie, who was an expert at dressage. Veronica came in third and Lisa placed fourth. The Saddle club managed to score enough points to compensate for Zach's early elimination.

At the end of the event Max called everybody together once again. "The overall winner of today's gymkhana is Group Three: Lisa, Carole, Stevie, and our newest member, Zach—who," he added, "should also receive a special congratulations for his spectacular performance today. Well done, 'Z.' "

Carole chuckled. Max had obviously picked up on Zach's habit of shortening Carole's name to C. She was enormously relieved to have won at least one event. It helped offset her two other miserable performances.

"We couldn't have done it without you," Stevie told Zach.

"You're going to be a great rider," Lisa said with open admiration.

Even Max praised the boy. "I've rarely seen such natural ability, Zach. Or such ragged form," he added with a grin. "Still, considering the short time you say you've been riding, today was very impressive."

Carole walked away, feeling left out. Normally Stevie and Lisa would have been congratulating her. She had, after all, won the last event for them. Today, however, no one seemed to care about anything except Zach's performance. As she stood apart from the crowd she noticed Barq, also alone and abandoned, tied to a rail. It was obviously going to be a while before the new star could tear himself away from his admirers. She went to the horse and stroked his forehead. "Just because your rider hasn't learned to put your needs first is no reason why you should suffer," she said, untying the horse. "Come on, boy. I'll take care of you."

After leading both Starlight and Barq back to the stables, Carole quietly groomed and watered them. As she was finishing, Lisa and Stevie showed up.

"Where have you been?" Lisa asked. "It's almost like a party out there."

"Yeah," agreed Stevie. "Zach's been telling us stories about his summer in Texas. It must've been a blast."

"Sorry I missed it," Carole replied insincerely. "Someone had to look after the horses."

"Good point," agreed Lisa. "I guess we'd better get started, too."

The two girls moved away.

"Oh!" Lisa cried. "We almost forgot to tell you."

Carole looked up expectantly.

"We invited Zach to have lunch with us on the knoll. He's going to tell us some more stories."

"He's such a crack-up!" added Stevie.

Carole felt annoyed. Lisa and Stevie were supposed to be her best friends, but they had almost forgotten to tell her about lunch because they were so swept off their feet by that boy.

"Sounds nice," she said with zero enthusiasm. "But, you know, I've got an awful lot of work left to do. Maybe you'd better start without me. I'll join you when I can."

"Okay," Stevie said. "See you later." She and Lisa departed, laughing over something funny Zach had told them.

They were actually leaving! Carole couldn't believe

it. Normally if she told them she was busy, they would have offered to help, but today they weren't giving her a thought.

Carole left Starlight's stall to go mix some grain for Sunset. Let them have their dumb old picnic. She wouldn't dream of turning up and spoiling the fun. That would show them.

LATER THAT AFTERNOON as she circled the ring with the rest of the class, Carole felt her spirits rising. She was performing much better than she had earlier in the day. Starlight's steady rhythm and the bright sunshine were a soothing balm to her ruffled feelings. Besides, she always enjoyed the afternoon class because Max tended to concentrate on the more technical aspects of riding.

"Zach," Max called, "you're still coming out of the saddle too high. And get those heels down!"

Carole felt a twinge of satisfaction. While Zach might be a whiz at galloping around pell-mell, he seemed to be having trouble mastering the finer points of the sport. From what she'd observed he didn't seem capable of concentrating on more than one instruction at a time. As soon as Max gave him additional skills to work on, the earlier instructions seemed to go right out of his head. She stole a glance at his face. He looked frustrated and unhappy. She remembered how joyful and enthusiastic he had been that morning and suddenly she didn't feel quite so self-satisfied.

"All right, everyone, come to the center," Max called.

Obediently the class pulled up their horses and approached him. "You're all doing very well. However, in order to keep you on your toes, I have arranged for us to compete in a small Pony Club schooling show two weeks from today."

A thrill of excitement ran through the riders.

"What other teams are competing, Max?" Stevie asked.

"Sunny Meadows and Cross County."

"Yes!" Stevie exclaimed. Her boyfriend, Phil, was a member of the Cross County Pony Club.

Max smiled. "I sort of thought you'd feel that way, Stevie."

"Excuse me, Max," Zach said. "What exactly is a schooling show?"

Max eyed the group. "Anyone care to fill him in?"

Lisa spoke up. "Sometimes some of the clubs get

together and compete in classes to see how we're all doing compared to each other. It's not officially recognized by the Horse Show Association, but it's a very useful learning tool."

"And lots of fun," Stevie added. "They usually have a choice of about ten classes you can enter. Jumping, pleasure, dressage, halter—that sort of thing."

"At various levels of experience, of course," Max assured Zach. "The judges will be me and the other two Pony Club directors. With that goal in mind, I think it might be useful for you to get a few extra lessons under your belt." He smiled at the boy. "How about it, Zach? Would you be interested in some private tutoring with me?"

Carole was amazed. Max was a very busy man and he rarely offered any of his students private sessions. She was certain the boy wouldn't appreciate the honor he was being offered.

To his credit, Zach looked enthusiastic. "Of course! That would mean extra time on horseback, right?"

"Yes, our lessons will be mounted," Max assured him. "However, it occurs to me you could use some help in other areas as well. There's a lot of preparation that goes into getting ready for a show." He scanned the other riders. "Does anybody want to volunteer to do a little tutoring?"

Stevie's and Lisa's hands immediately shot up.

"We'd be happy to help Zach," Stevie said.

"Absolutely," Lisa concurred. "How about it, Carole?"

Carole felt Max's eyes turn to her. For the first time in her life she found herself reluctant to help someone. Only this morning she had told herself that she would give Zach some pointers, but that had been before all the big fuss over his riding ability. Zach would do fine without her. After all, he had Stevie and Lisa falling all over themselves to work with him. "I think I'm going to leave it up to you two this time," she said, not meeting Stevie's and Lisa's eyes. "I have a lot of extra work looking after Sunset, and I think she deserves my full attention."

"I'm sure Sunset will benefit greatly from your care," Max told her, turning away.

"Carole, you're not going to be too busy for our trail ride tomorrow, are you?" Stevie asked anxiously.

Carole broke into a smile. A ride with her two best friends was exactly what she needed to shake off this mood. "Of course not. You can definitely count on me for that."

Stevie looked relieved. "Great, because we told Zach we would show him our favorite spot by the creek."

Carole felt her spirits plummet. They had invited Zach to go with them! She had planned to talk to Stevie and Lisa about her feelings toward him, but now she wouldn't be able to. Worse, he would probably do something spectacular and blow everybody away again. Did she really want to see that? No way! Would anybody miss her if she didn't go? Doubtful. Could she think of a way to gracefully excuse herself? Negative.

She would simply have to make the best of it.

"Tell you what," Max was saying. "You all did such a fine job this morning that I'm going to end class with a few minutes of free riding around the ring. When you're done, take care of your horses and I'll see you all next time." He started to move away. "Carole, you're in charge."

"Okay, Max." His confidence in her made her feel much better. She urged Starlight into a rocking canter, leading the others around the ring. After a couple of circles she signaled Stevie to take the point and trotted into the middle of the ring to keep an eye on the others. Zach had a broad grin on his face once again, clearly having the time of his life. Carole knew how he felt. The speed and strength of the animal beneath her was always a rush. Sometimes the responsibilities of riding weighed her down and she forgot the sheer joy of simply being one with her horse. Watching Zach, she was reminded of what it was that had first attracted her to the sport, and to her surprise, she found herself smiling as she watched him.

What is my problem? she wondered. Zach was a nice guy. Stevie and Lisa liked him, and they had good instincts. Actually *everybody* seemed to like him. Could it be she was jealous of all the attention he'd been getting? Could she really be that petty? Suddenly she felt ashamed. Zach had done nothing wrong. In fact he'd saved the day for The Saddle Club; and how was she repaying him? By refusing to help him. She decided that would stop right then. From that moment on she would do everything she could to encourage him to grow in the sport.

"Okay, everybody, time's up," she called.

There were several groans of protest, including a few from Zach, but everybody reined in and walked their horses out of the ring.

Carole dismounted Starlight and waited for Stevie and Lisa to join her. Zach was tagging along.

"That was a tough class," he said. "I liked the last few minutes the best."

"I know what you mean," Stevie said. "Sometimes it's fun to let your horse out."

"Not sometimes, *all* the time," Zach replied with a

grin. "I don't think my cousin and I ever went any-where slower than a gallop."

Carole cringed. "Fun for you, but kind of hard on your horses, don't you think?"

"Don't worry, C, I'm exaggerating," Zach assured her. "Actually Turbo, the horse I was riding there, was truly cool and I tried to look out for him. You know, like you do for a friend. Now, I've got Barq here," he added, patting his horse's neck. "If we're going to be buds, then I'd better learn to take care of him, too."

Carole was tremendously relieved to hear that. Perhaps she had been too hasty to judge him after all.

Lisa smiled at him approvingly. "Good attitude, Zach."

"You know, after a long day of riding, sometimes I like to go home and soak in a bath." Carole mused.

"Oh, I know what you mean," Lisa agreed whole-heartedly. "I could soak for hours."

Stevie let out a bitter laugh. "Ha! Never happen in my house. I'm lucky if my brothers give me five min-utes. After that, it's pure grief."

Lisa giggled. "She suffers terribly."

Carole laughed, too. "Joan of Arc has nothing on our Stevie."

"I'm more of a shower man myself," said Zach. "Mr. Efficient."

Carole had hoped he'd say something like that. It was the opportunity she was looking for. "Funny you should say that, Zach, because I think Barq feels the same way."

"Huh? You have a shower for horses around here?"

"We have the next best thing," Carole assured him. "We have a hose."

"That's a great idea, Carole," Lisa said. "Let's give the horses a bath. They've worked hard today."

"Sure, they deserve it," Stevie agreed.

Zach looked from one girl to another. "Back in Texas we brushed the horses, but I don't remember ever washing them."

Lisa smiled. "Well then, Zach, allow us to introduce you to a new experience."

"You know, you haven't really lived until you've washed under a horse's tail," Stevie told him with a big grin.

Zach pulled a face of disgust and for a moment Carole thought he was going to refuse. Then he laughed.

"I guess my cousin was holding out on me. Okay, if you guys will show me how, I'm game."

The four of them removed their horses' saddles and bridles and slipped on their halters. Over the next hour the girls proceeded to show Zach how to thoroughly wash a horse.

Carole watched the boy closely as he learned how to carefully sponge off Barq's face. He was surprisingly gentle cleaning out the horse's nostrils and the corners of his eyes. Although he was a bit clumsy with some of the equipment, dropping the hoof pick a couple of times, even Carole had to admit he seemed completely devoted to making sure Barq got the care the animal deserved.

By the time the four of them were finished, the horses were shining from head to toe and the humans were exhausted.

Zach sank down onto a hay bale. "I'm wiped. Please, please tell me we don't have to do that every time we ride!"

"Nah," Stevie assured him. "Only every other time."

Zach looked dismayed.

"Actually it's more like every now and then," Lisa assured him. "Stevie's pulling your leg."

"Could you pull off my boots while you're at it?" he asked Stevie. "My feet are killing me."

Carole spotted Max coming across the stable yard. "Hey, guys, I suggest we beat a hasty retreat before Max assigns us chores."

"Chores!" exclaimed Zach, jumping up. "Color me gone!"

As a rule Max took advantage of kids hanging

around the stable by putting them to work. This helped cut down on expenses so that he could keep his riding rates lower and more people could afford to learn. Usually The Saddle Club didn't mind helping out, but just then they were exhausted.

Moving quickly to collect their things, they managed to slip out of Pine Hollow without Max spotting them.

"Don't forget about the trail ride," Lisa reminded Zach as they were about to part company.

"Wouldn't miss it," Zach assured her. "Tomorrow I'll show you some real riding!"

4

THE NEXT DAY the weather was glorious, perfect for a trail ride. Carole watched as cotton-ball clouds drifted through the blue skies. "I can't remember a more perfect-looking day."

"It really is the best time of year for riding," Stevie said from her place in line.

"I hope it's like this for the day of the show," Lisa said.

"Speaking of which . . ." Stevie turned in her saddle to look behind her. "What classes do you think you'll enter, Zach?"

"Don't know," he replied thoughtfully. "All of them, I guess."

From the moment they set out on their ride, Zach

had been smiling contentedly, and Carole could tell he was enjoying the informal atmosphere and the camaraderie. She also couldn't help noticing that his heels were up and his elbows were sticking out. He really was going to need to put in some hard work before the competition.

"You can't enter them all," Stevie laughed. "Only the ones for your experience level."

Zach frowned. "I wish I didn't have to ride in the baby classes."

"That's *beginner* classes. Of which you are one," Carole reminded him.

"But everyone keeps telling me I'm good," he protested.

"Oh you are, Zach," Stevie assured him. "I've never seen anyone as good as you with so little experience."

"But in competition, details are hugely important," Lisa said solemnly.

"Like heels and elbows," Carole added pointedly.

Zach took the hint and corrected his posture. Carole smiled.

"Maybe you should start with the halter class," Stevie suggested.

"What's that?"

"That's where you show your horse in only his

45

halter," Lisa told him. "You'll be judged on his conformation—"

"His what?"

"You know, how he's built. Does he stand with his legs squarely under himself or is he slouching? When you ask him to move out do you have to tug on his lead line or does he obey you right away? That kind of thing."

Zach made a face. "Boring!"

"What about dressage?" Stevie said. "That's one of my favorites."

"Go on . . . ," Zach said.

"It's only you and your horse in the ring. You have to perform certain precise movements and the judges score you on how well you do them."

Zach looked doubtful. "What kind of movements?"

"Side passes, moving from a collected trot to an extended one, that kind of thing. And the judges shouldn't see you giving cues to your horse. It should almost look like you're doing nothing and the horse is doing everything."

Zach looked completely uninterested. "Or I could sit and watch cement dry."

Carole saw Stevie was a little hurt. "It takes a great deal of skill to compete in dressage, Zach. As a matter of fact, Stevie is one of the very best at it."

Stevie smiled at her. "Thanks."

"I have a feeling Zach is looking for something with more action," Lisa said.

"You should learn to jump, Zach," Stevie suggested enthusiastically. "It's absolutely the best. You canter up to a fence and the next thing you know you're soaring over it. It's awesome."

That seemed to get his attention. "Now we're talking!"

"Of course it will be a little while before you're ready for that," Carole cautioned. "Not in time for this show, certainly."

Zach looked discouraged. "Do they have anything with galloping?"

Carole shook her head. "I'm afraid you're out of luck. Most saddle classes are restricted to walking, trotting, and cantering, although sometimes they ask for a hand gallop."

"What's a hand gallop?"

"That means it's very controlled," Lisa told him. "Anyway, I wouldn't count on it. They don't usually ask for it in the novice classes."

Carole considered the possibilities the show would offer. "The serpentine class is ridden at a canter."

"That sounds cool."

"Can you do a flying lead change?" Lisa asked.

"What?"

Stevie smiled knowingly. "The class is about weaving your horse through a series of standing poles while at the canter, but the really tricky part is getting the horse to change leads every time he goes around one. We call that a flying lead change."

"And a lead would be *what*, exactly?"

"When a horse canters, one of his front legs strikes the ground first," Carole explained. "If it's his right leg, then he's on a right lead; if it's his left leg, then he's—"

"On his left lead," Zach finished for her. "I think I could handle that."

"We can go over the list of classes when we get back to the stable," Carole offered. "Maybe then you'll get an idea of what you're interested in."

"Oh, I know what I'm into," he said, grinning. "I feel the need for speed. Wouldn't this be a perfect place for a gallop?"

They were entering a grassy open field. The Saddle Club had been through it dozens of times, so they knew it was perfectly safe to let the horses out.

"We usually stick to a canter when we're on a trail ride," Carole said cautiously.

"Oh come on, C, lighten up," he coaxed.

"I think it would be okay for a little bit," Stevie said.

"Are you up for it, Lisa?" Carole asked.

48

Lisa nodded.

"Okay," Carole agreed.

Even as the words left her mouth, Zach yelled, "Yahoo!" and kicked Barq into a gallop. The three girls were a little startled. Since Zach wasn't familiar with the terrain, it would have been wiser for one of them to lead the way. With no alternative, the three of them went after him.

Feeling the rush of the wind in her face, Carole leaned forward, urging Starlight to go faster. He snorted and responded with a burst of speed. Up ahead she could see Zach as he raced along. His riding showed not a drop of style, but she had to admit that he had a great seat and seemed absolutely fearless.

Stevie pulled even with her and the two of them shared a smile. Galloping was fun but it could also be dangerous, and a fall at this speed could have serious consequences. Carole decided they had better slow down. She managed to close the distance between her and the racing boy. "Zach!" she yelled. "Hold up!"

With obvious reluctance Zach reined Barq to a halt. The horse bounced around on his feet, too wound up from the run to stand completely still. Carole noticed Zach was having a hard time holding him in place.

Smiling and breathless, Stevie and Lisa joined them. Their faces were flushed and their eyes glittering from the sting of the wind.

"That was great!" Zach enthused.

Stevie smiled happily and flicked a strand of loose hair from her eyes. "We should do that more often."

"No time like the present," Zach yelled, and before the girls could protest, he was galloping away.

Carole was dismayed. "This is not good."

Lisa looked anxious. "That field gets rough farther on. He could get hurt."

"Not to mention Barq," Stevie added. "Come on!"

The three girls urged their horses back into a gallop using all their skills to shorten the distance between themselves and Zach. Fueled by the possible urgency of the situation, Carole managed to coax some extra speed from Starlight. Finally she found herself within earshot to the speeding rider. "Zach, stop!" she shouted.

Zach looked surprised to find her so close to him.

"Pull up!" she cried urgently.

Something in her voice must have got through to him because he immediately slowed Barq down and gradually came to a halt.

"Phew, that was close," Stevie said as she rode up on a winded Belle.

"What's up?" Zach asked impatiently. "How come we're stopping so soon?"

"Zach, you can't simply go galloping through places

you don't know!" Carole scolded him. "It's not safe for you or your horse."

"It looks fine," he protested.

"Well it's not," Lisa assured him. "A couple of yards from here the field gets bumpy and rocky. You can't see it because of the grass, but the horses could easily hurt themselves."

"Not to mention you could take a serious dive," Stevie added grimly.

Zach looked contrite. "Sorry. Guess I got carried away."

Carole sighed. After all, he was new to the rules of riding. "Never mind. Let's go on to the creek." Then she added firmly, "At a leisurely walk." Although he was obviously disappointed, Zach obeyed and the rest of the trip was uneventful.

Once down by the creek the girls immediately stripped off their boots and socks and dangled their feet in the cool water. As usual the talk drifted to the subject of horses.

"Hey, Zach, come and join us," Lisa called.

Zach sat in the grass beside them.

"Take off your boots," Stevie urged. "The water's great."

"Nah, then I'd have to wait for my feet to dry before I could put them back on."

"So?"

"I didn't think we were going to be here that long."

Carole saw his eyes stray longingly toward the horses. The beauty of the spot was wasted on him. It was obvious he was eager to get back in the saddle, not sit and talk. "We have to give the horses a chance to cool off, Zach," she said, "but then we can get going."

Stevie also seemed to have picked up on his restlessness. "Why don't you go see how they're doing while we dry our feet," she suggested.

Zach jumped up eagerly. "Okay."

"Do you know how to tell if Barq is cooled down?" Lisa asked before he could run off.

Zach shrugged. "If he's not sweating?"

"Actually, you put your hand on his chest. If it's not hot then he's ready to be ridden again."

"You guys sure do know a lot about horses," he said as he moved off.

Carole shook her head and reached for her socks. "I've never seen anyone so keen to be in the saddle."

"He's definitely eager to learn," Stevie agreed.

That wasn't what Carole had meant at all. While Zach obviously loved riding, he didn't seem to enjoy the process of learning what went with it. Still, he was new to the sport and probably overwhelmed by all the information he was getting, so she decided to keep her thoughts to herself.

"Barq is nice and cool, guys," he called, "and so are your horses."

Lisa laughed. "I think that's a hint."

"Come on, girls," Stevie said, standing up. "This kind of devotion to horses should be nurtured."

"But my feet aren't even dry," Lisa protested.

"Dry them with your socks," Stevie suggested. "I did."

Lisa wrinkled her nose. "Then I'll have wet socks. It'll feel like my feet are all sweaty."

Stevie shrugged. "What's your point?"

"It's gross, that's my point!"

"Come on, Lisa," Carole coaxed. "If we don't get Zach back on his horse soon, I think he'll go into withdrawal."

Lisa looked over to where the boy was pacing back and forth and throwing the girls anxious looks. "Okay, okay," she relented.

The girls quickly finished getting ready, and the four of them mounted up to continue their ride. Stevie was in the lead, Lisa right behind her, Zach next, and Carole brought up the rear.

Carole thought the new rider might be a little anxious about the upcoming show, so she decided to give him some reassurance. "You know, Zach, even though you only have a few weeks of riding experience, I think you're going to do fine at the show. It really isn't all that important, anyway."

Zach turned and smiled at her. "Oh, I know that, C, but it's still going to be cool to hang a handful of ribbons on my wall."

Stevie laughed. "Gee, too bad you suffer from such low self-confidence."

Carole didn't find it particularly funny. In fact she was somewhat put off by the boy's cocky attitude. "You do realize not everybody wins their first time out, don't you?"

Zach shrugged. "I know that, but Max said I have great potential as a rider, so I'll just do what comes naturally. I can't lose."

Carole shook her head. She didn't want to discourage him, but—

"Hey, Zach," Stevie called, turning in her saddle, "remind me to—"

She never got any further. At that moment a fox streaked across the path practically under Belle's feet. While the mare was normally the steadiest and most reliable of mounts, millions of years of instinct took over. She shied hard to the left, catching

Stevie off guard and off balance. With a shout of surprise she was thrown from her saddle, hitting the ground hard.

Belle, still alarmed by the fox, took off at a panicked gallop.

"Stevie!" Lisa cried, dismounting quickly and rushing over to her fallen friend. "Are you hurt?"

Carole and Zach also hurried over.

Stevie was sitting in the dirt looking dazed. "I'm okay. . . . I think. Good thing I was wearing this."

She gingerly removed her riding helmet, which had gotten knocked askew in the fall.

Lisa frowned, her face full of concern. "Looks like you got a nice bump even so."

Zach knelt beside her. "Man, that looked rough. Are you okay, Stevie?"

Stevie saw that her fall had shaken Zach almost as much as her. "Don't worry about it, Zach. If you're going to ride horses, sooner or later you're going to fall off. The trick is getting back on." She looked around anxiously. "Where's Belle?"

"She ran off," Carole said. "I wanted to make sure you were all right before I went after her."

"I'm okay," Stevie insisted. "Please find her. She was scared and could get hurt!"

Carole thought her friend was looking awfully pale.

"Don't worry, I'll find her." She turned to Lisa and Zach. "You two look after Stevie. I'll be back as soon as I can."

It didn't take Carole long to locate Belle. The horse was standing by the edge of the woods, her reins dangling on the ground. She pricked her ears and nickered when she saw Carole on Starlight. Carole dismounted and slowly approached, talking soothingly. Belle stood docilely, making no attempt to get away.

As soon as Carole gathered up Belle's reins and began to lead her back to the others, she noticed the horse was favoring her right foreleg. She knew a horse's legs were delicate and susceptible to all kinds of injury, especially from the knee down. She knelt for a closer look and was alarmed to discover a definite swelling around the fetlock. Although Carole would have preferred not to move the mare until she knew the extent of the injury, she didn't have much choice: She had to get back to Stevie.

Picking the easiest path and moving as slowly as she could, she returned to where Stevie was sitting on the ground under the shade of a tree.

Lisa came to meet her. "I think Stevie may have a concussion," she said in a hushed voice.

Carole was immediately concerned. "What makes you think so?"

"When she stood up she got dizzy. She said things were kind of sparkly, so we had her sit back down."

Carole felt her stomach tighten with anxiety. "That doesn't sound good. Belle is hurt, too. I don't know how badly, but I hate to move her until someone can take a look at it."

Zach joined the two girls. "What's up?"

"Belle is injured, too," Lisa told him quietly.

Carole bit her lip. "I wish Max were here."

"That's it!" Zach cried. "I know how to get back to the stable. You two stay here with Stevie and I'll bring back help." He rushed over to where he had tied Barq and leaped into the saddle. "Back in a flash!" he assured them.

"Wait!" Carole cried, alarmed at the idea of his galloping all the way to Pine Hollow, but she was too late. Zach was already urging his horse into a run.

"Gosh, I hope he doesn't get hurt," Lisa said.

Carole was also concerned. "Me too. Come on, let's go sit with Stevie. All we can do now is wait for a rescue."

Lisa watched as Zach vanished around the bend at a blazing gallop. "At least he'll get there fast."

"If he gets there at all," Carole said grimly.

5

STEVIE WATCHED BELLE with grave concern. She was much more worried about her horse than herself. "How bad do you think she's hurt?"

Carole sighed. "I really can't tell. There are several possibilities. But I don't think it's too serious—she's favoring the leg but she doesn't seem to be in a lot of pain."

Stevie's head hurt and she felt like crying. "I'll never forgive myself if it's serious. I should have been paying attention to the trail, not gabbing."

Lisa slid a comforting arm around her shoulders. "We always chat when we ride. You were just unlucky today, that's all."

"Lisa's right," Carole agreed. "It could have happened to any one of us, and if that fox had jumped out at

58

Starlight, he would have reacted the same way Belle did."

"The difference is you wouldn't have fallen off," Stevie said despondently.

"I've taken my share of spills," Carole reminded her.

"Me too," Lisa admitted. "In fact, you've been there for most of them."

Stevie mustered a smile. "And vice versa."

Carole frowned. "Speaking of falls, I hope our fearless would-be hero doesn't take one."

"Try not to worry. I'm sure he made it to the stables okay." Lisa said. "In fact, he could be back with Max any time now."

Almost as if he had heard their conversation, Zach appeared from around the bend riding Barq at a canter. Much to the girls' mutual relief, Max was right behind.

Max immediately dismounted and hurried to where Stevie sat. "Zach told me you took quite the tumble," he said, kneeling down next to her.

Stevie felt foolish. She hated it when she fell. Not so much for the pain, but because she felt like it made her look like less of a rider. "It wasn't so spectacular."

Max raised his eyebrows in mock surprise. "Modesty from you, Stevie? Now I really *am* alarmed. Let me take a look at your head."

Stevie squirmed. "I'm okay, Max, it's Belle who's hurt. Could you please check on her?"

"Stevie, you know how strongly I feel about horses, but people come first," he said firmly. "Now tell me how you're feeling. Are you nauseous or dizzy?"

"She said she was dizzy when she tried to stand up," Lisa volunteered.

Max nodded. "How's your vision?"

"I saw stars at first. Now things just look a little fuzzy around the edges," Stevie confessed. She was glad to have an adult around to take charge. Truth was, she didn't feel all that great and was a little scared.

Max took her head between his hands. "Let me look into your eyes." After a moment he seemed satisfied and released her. "I would guess that you have a mild concussion. Nothing to be alarmed about, but you'll have to go to the hospital for a checkup just to be on the safe side."

Stevie nodded her consent. "Now will you look at Belle?" she pleaded.

Max smiled and touched her gently on the cheek. "Yes, now I'll look at Belle." He picked up a backpack he had brought with him and approached the horse. Belle looked alert but was holding her foreleg slightly off the ground. He knelt down and gently ran his hand down the leg. Belle twitched uneasily.

Stevie winced in sympathy with her.

"Do you think it's serious, Max?" Carole asked.

"Any injury to a horse's leg should be taken seriously," Max replied, continuing his examination. "It could be a sprain of the fetlock joint or the tendon. It's difficult to tell with this much swelling."

Stevie struggled not to cry. "How will we get her home? Can she walk on it?"

Max opened the bundle. "We're going to have to apply a pressure bandage. That should give her enough support to make it back to the stable."

They all watched closely as he placed thick cotton wadding evenly around the leg. "This cotton will keep the bandages from injuring her skin. Carole, can you hold it in place while I wrap?"

Carole did as he asked.

Max carefully wound the long crepe bandage around Belle's leg, making sure it covered well above and below the actual injured area, and pulled it as tightly as he could. "It's too bad we can't hose it down with cool water first," he said as he worked. "That often helps reduce the swelling in these situations."

When he was finished he stepped back to study his work, then had Carole lead the mare forward a few steps while he observed. Belle still favored the leg but didn't seem quite as distressed about putting weight on it as she had before.

Max returned to Stevie and the others. "If we take it nice and slow she should make it back to the stable without any problem. Before Zach and I left, I asked Mrs. Reg to call Judy Barker and your parents, Stevie. They'll probably be there by the time we arrive."

Stevie started to climb to her feet. For a moment the world swirled dizzily around her. If it hadn't been for Lisa and Max steadying her, she might have fallen again.

"Take it easy," Max warned. "Normally it's a good idea to get back in the saddle right after a fall. In this case, however, I'd prefer you didn't."

"Why do you have to get right back up on a horse when you fall?" Zach whispered to Lisa.

"The idea is to not give yourself too much time to think about what happened," she explained. "If you do, you could lose your nerve."

"On the other hand," Max continued, "you're in no condition to walk all the way back."

Stevie agreed. She really didn't feel much like walking, but it was an unwritten rule of riding that you always put your horse's needs before your own. "I have to lead Belle home," she said determinedly.

"I can do that," Carole volunteered, "and you can ride Starlight. He's very steady."

Max nodded. "Good idea, Carole. Thanks for offering." He turned back to Stevie. "Now let's get you up and back to Pine Hollow. No arguments."

Although Stevie's head swam a little when she first mounted Starlight, she was okay once she was up.

The little group began the long, slow trip back home.

Stevie was relieved when she finally spotted the stable. As Max had predicted, she saw her family's car parked in the driveway.

Max helped her dismount. Even before her feet touched the ground, her parents were beside her, hugging her tightly.

"Stevie, honey, are you all right?"

Stevie was embarrassed by the fuss. "Sure, Mom, it was only a little fall. No big deal, happens all the time."

" 'Happens all the time' is not exactly what we want to hear, sweetheart," her father scolded her gently. "I think we'll take you over to the hospital for a checkup."

Stevie was too tired to argue. "Okay, Dad. But what about Belle?"

"Don't worry," Lisa assured her. "We'll take care of her until Judy can get here."

Stevie smiled wearily, knowing she could count on her friends. She walked over to where the mare stood patiently, planted a gentle kiss on her velvet-soft nose, then slipped her arms around her neck. "I'm sorry, Belle," she whispered, close to tears.

After a moment she felt her dad's hand on her shoulder. "Come on, honey, time to go."

They headed for the car.

"Call us when you know something, okay?" Lisa yelled.

Stevie waved and nodded, then slid gratefully into the backseat and closed her eyes.

It wasn't far to the hospital, but there was a long wait in the emergency room. Stevie spent the time fretting over Belle. She knew everyone at Pine Hollow would do their best for the horse, but not knowing the extent of her mare's injury was really distressing her. After what seemed like hours, her name was finally called.

Dr. Laurie Trudell had kind dark eyes and a friendly smile. She checked Stevie over thoroughly, including looking at her eyes, cleaning up her bump, and asking her questions about the accident.

Finally the doctor turned to Mr. and Mrs. Lake. "I'm satisfied that your daughter hasn't suffered any major trauma. She's got a mild concussion, though, and you'll need to watch her closely for a few days.

Her parents looked relieved.

"Just to play it safe, I want to send her down the hall for a CAT scan. After we get the results, you can probably take her home."

"Not home," Stevie protested. "I have to get back to the stables."

"You've done all the riding you're going to do for a few days," the doctor told her sternly. "You need to go to bed."

"Please, doctor," she pleaded passionately. "I have to check on Belle."

"Belle?" Dr. Trudell looked inquiringly at Mr. and Mrs. Lake.

"That's her horse," Mrs. Lake explained.

Stevie was racked by worry and guilt. "She was hurt, too, and it's my fault because I wasn't paying attention. Please, I need to check on her." The room was getting blurry around her but it wasn't from the concussion, it was from the tears in her eyes.

Dr. Trudell smiled slightly. "I can see you take your responsibilities to your horse very seriously, which says a lot about your character. I'll tell you what: If your CAT scan comes back clean, you have my permission to stop by and check on Belle."

Stevie's heart leaped with gratitude.

"But"—the doctor held up a warning finger—"only for a few minutes. After that it's home and right to bed."

Her parents nodded their agreement.

Contented now, Stevie wiped her eyes and blew her nose. She couldn't wait to get back to Pine Hollow.

STEVIE WAS OUT of the car almost before it had stopped. She was dismayed to see Judy Barker's light blue pickup in front of the stables, and her stomach clenched. If the veterinarian was still there, then Belle's injury must have been a lot worse than Max had thought.

She hurried into the stable and directly to the mare's stall, where she spotted Carole putting some of Judy's equipment back into the medical kit.

"How is she, Carole?" Stevie asked, almost sick with worry.

"Stevie?" Carole cried, her eyes wide with surprise. "What are you doing here? Shouldn't you be at the hospital?"

"I'm fine, only a little concussion like Max thought. I can't ride for a while, though," she added gloomily.

66

"I'm sorry to hear that, but I'm glad you're okay. I was worried about you. We all were, even Zach."

Stevie was touched by everyone's concern, but she really had to find out about her horse. "How's Belle?"

"Mind if I field that one, Carole?" Judy asked, rising up from inside the mare's stall.

"Sorry, Judy, I didn't see you in there." Stevie moved to join the veterinarian inside. To her it looked like nothing had changed since she'd left. The mare still wore a neat white bandage on her foreleg, which she continued to hold slightly off the ground. "How's she doing?"

"She's going to be fine," Judy assured her, patting the mare gently on the neck. "Max did the right thing by applying the pressure bandage. There's no permanent injury."

Stevie felt her body sag with relief. She leaned her cheek against Belle's warm neck and gave her a hug. "Boy, am I glad to hear that. I've been really worried about you, girl."

"Your horse has a sprained tendon," Judy explained. "She probably stumbled and caught herself when she got away from you. It's a fairly common injury, especially in the forelegs, because they're more delicate but still have to carry the majority of the horse's weight—head, neck, shoulders. Fortunately Belle's injury isn't severe."

Lisa had joined Carole at the stall door. "Now for the bad news," she said. "Judy says you won't be able to ride her for at least two, maybe even three weeks."

Stevie's heart sank. "But the show is in two weeks!"

"Sorry, kiddo," Judy said, "but you should be grateful it won't be longer than that. I've seen horses with this kind of injury take up to six weeks to get sound again."

"Bad luck," Carole commiserated.

Stevie was disappointed, but at least Belle was going to be all right. "That's okay. Like Judy said, it could have been worse."

Lisa looked sad. "It won't be the same without you competing."

Stevie shrugged, determined to make the best of it. "On the plus side, this means I'll have more time to coach Zach."

Lisa brightened. "With his riding and your coaching, I predict two weeks from now Pine Hollow will rule!"

Stevie noticed Carole was giving them a skeptical look. "Do you doubt?" she asked her.

"How could he possibly fail?" Carole replied with little enthusiasm.

Stevie was about to question her friend further when she heard her mother calling. She quickly gave her horse one last pat, thanked Judy, and headed gratefully for home. Whatever was bothering Carole would have to wait.

CAROLE DOUBLE-CHECKED the supply of fresh bandages in the veterinary cupboard. For the next week, at least, Belle's leg would need to be massaged every morning and night and then re-bound, so she wanted to be sure they had enough supplies on hand.

At the same time she checked the foaling supplies they would need for Sunset's delivery. Tail bandages, head collars, feeding bottles, milk replacer . . . By the time she had worked her way through the inventory, she was satisfied they would be able to handle any emergency that might arise.

Although Sunset had shown no signs that she was ready to give birth anytime soon, Carole decided to look in on the mare anyway. The horse was not in her stall, so she checked the small private paddock out back. She spotted the mare in the far corner of the enclosed space and slowly approached. "Hey, girl, what are you up to?"

As she got closer she could see something was wrong—not with the horse, but with the fence. The wood was chipped away and splintered. One of the boards had actually cracked, as if the mare had been kicking and pawing at it.

Worried by Sunset's behavior, she led the mare back into her stall and shut the door to the paddock, then went to find Red O'Malley, the head stable hand. Red was working in the barn.

"Hi, Red," she called.

"Oh, hi, Carole," he greeted her with a friendly smile. "I thought you'd be long gone by now."

"I was about to take off, but when I checked on Sunset I discovered she'd been trying to run away."

Red stopped working. "Run away? How?"

"She's been pawing and leaning on the fence to her paddock. She's actually managed to break one of the boards."

Red frowned. "That can be dangerous. I'd better take a look at it. Thanks for letting me know." He set off across the yard.

Carole went with him. "Red, do all pregnant mares

behave like that, or do you think something's wrong with her?"

"Lots of changes happen when a mare is this far along," he explained. "Most of them become antisocial, then nervous. The fact that Sunset is away from home in unfamiliar surroundings makes it all the harder for her. Most likely she wanted more privacy, or maybe she just wanted to explore." He shrugged. "It's hard to say."

"Then you don't think it's something to worry about?"

"I doubt it." He let himself into the stall. Sunset was standing in a corner with her back to them. "You know, most horses manage foaling with very little trouble. It's the people who care about them that have the difficulty." He winked at her. "Don't worry so much. I think she's fine."

Carole smiled. "Thanks, Red."

He gave her a thumbs-up and disappeared into the paddock.

Reassured by his words, Carole moved closer to the mare to stroke her. "Is that it, girl?" she crooned gently. "Are you just nervous? You don't have to be scared. I'm not going to let anything bad happen to you or your baby."

For her part, Sunset seemed entirely indifferent to Carole's assurances and caresses. She tolerated them for a moment or two, then moved restlessly away to begin the laborious process of lying down. With much grunting and groaning she managed to lower herself onto the soft hay.

"I guess I can take a hint," Carole told the horse. "You obviously don't care for any company."

The mare closed her eyes.

Carole checked the water and food. "Okay, I'm leaving now."

Sunset gave a soft snort, but Carole was almost certain it was meant to be a fake snore.

"No, no, don't get up, I think I can find my way out," she said, laughing. "See you tomorrow, girl."

She latched the stall door carefully and headed for home.

THE NEXT AFTERNOON the Saddle Club members all arrived at Pine Hollow at practically the same moment.

"Hi, Stevie," Lisa called. "Are you feeling better?"

"Yeah, how's the bump?" Carole asked.

"Beats a poke in the eye with a sharp stick," she told them, smiling. "Then again, what doesn't?"

Lisa laughed. "Healthy attitude."

The sound of hoofbeats drew Carole's attention to the outdoor ring. "What's up over there?"

"Looks like Zach is taking a lesson with Max,"

Stevie said. "He's one of the reasons I came over today."

"Let's see how it's going," Lisa suggested.

"Oh, be still my heart," Carole mumbled, reluctantly trailing behind her friends. For reasons she could not figure out, she still felt distant from Zach. It was not that she didn't like him, but she definitely didn't get the same thrill from watching him ride that everybody else seemed to. As they approached, it became more and more obvious that Zach wasn't a happy camper.

"It's just not happening for me, Max," he complained loudly.

"You're going to have to give it time, Zach," Max counseled. "You're doing fine, but you can't expect to master it all in a day. It takes time."

Zach was frowning. "How much time?"

Max put his hands in his pockets. "I know people who have been riding their entire lives and they tell me they still learn something new every day."

"Maybe they're slow studies," Stevie cracked from her position on the fence.

Max glanced at her. "I see that knock on the head hasn't improved your jokes, Stevie."

Stevie feigned surprise. "Max, how can you improve on perfection?"

Zach laughed.

Max turned back to the boy. "That's better. You need to relax, be patient."

"I don't think patience is Zach's strong suit," Carole murmured to her friends.

"But I thought you said I was a natural," Zach complained to Max.

"You are," he assured him. "You have a rare gift and you owe it to yourself to nurture it."

Zach looked unconvinced. "I guess."

"I have to go now, but you can keep practicing if you want," Max told him. "We'll arrange for another lesson later in the week."

Carole felt a pang of jealousy. More private lessons! Zach sure was getting the golden-boy treatment.

Zach rode Barq over to the girls and casually slid down from the saddle. "Hi, guys. What's up?"

In spite of herself, Carole couldn't help admiring the unconscious grace of his movements. It took most people months, if not years, to learn to dismount a horse so fluidly.

"I thought maybe we could get in some practice for the show," Stevie suggested.

"Thanks, but Max beat you to it."

Lisa reached out to stroke Barq. "Sounded like you were having some problems."

"Yeah. It was kind of a drag. I think I'll call it quits for now."

"How long have you been out here?" Lisa asked.

Zach shrugged. "Almost an hour, I guess." He scuffed at the dirt. "Max didn't even let me gallop."

Carole was tempted to tell him there was a lot more to riding than galloping, but she held her tongue. She couldn't understand why he didn't seem to care about all the hundreds of details that went into making up a polished rider, or the thousands of details that it took to become a responsible horse owner. She'd spent countless hours studying and learning as much as she could about the subject. Zach, on the other hand, had probably spent endless hours playing video games. Instant gratification. Typical boy.

"An hour's not much practice time when you think about how close we are to the show," Lisa said, voicing Carole's thoughts. "Why don't you let us work with you for a while?"

"I don't know . . ."

"Come on, Zach," Stevie coaxed. "Since I can't ride for a while, you'd practically be doing me a favor."

Listening to Stevie trying to convince the boy into letting her help him really annoyed Carole. He should have been down on his hands and knees begging her, grateful for all the experience she was offering to share.

Zach relented. "Okay. You talked me in to it. On one condition."

"What's that," asked Stevie.

"I get to canter at least a couple of times during the lesson."

Stevie and Lisa laughed. "Agreed," they said in unison.

Stevie turned to Carole. "How about it, Carole, are you in on this?"

"Sorry, no can do," she begged off. "I have to check on Sunset."

"We'll see you later then," Stevie said. "Come on, Zach, tell us what you were having trouble with, and Lisa and I will try to figure out how to help."

Carole quickly made herself scarce, retiring to Sunset's stall. The mare was pacing restlessly, which was usually a sign that a horse wasn't ready to drop her foal yet. Carole decided a good grooming was in order.

She collected her equipment and, after carefully cross-tying Sunset, began to give her a thorough cleaning. From where she was working she could hear bits and pieces of what the others were up to outside in the ring.

"*Olé!*" Stevie shouted.

That was Carole's clue that they were working on a game called horseback bullfighting. Carole hadn't played it in a long time, but she remembered it was a fun way to practice turns on the forehand and the hindquarters. The idea was to have someone, on foot or mounted, trot toward you, aiming at your stirrup. At the last moment you have to move your horse's hindquarters out of the way without getting touched. As the fake bull goes by, you turn and face it, making a 180-degree turn like a bullfighter does.

"*Olé!*" Stevie cried again. "You're doing great, Zach!"

"You're doing great, Zach," Carole mimicked to herself. She tried to put the noise out of her mind and concentrate on what she was doing, but every time Lisa or Stevie showered Zach with praises, it made her grit her teeth.

Eager to get out of earshot, Carole hurried to complete the job. She was just finishing up when she heard Max outside. Figuring he had come to check on Zach's progress, she stopped working in order to listen to the conversation, certain that Max would not be as impressed with Zach's technique as Stevie and Lisa obviously were.

"It looks like you've made some good strides," Max called to the boy.

"This is fun," Zach yelled back. "It's not even like working."

"Nice job, Stevie," Max said. "I've been trying to get him to do those moves for an hour, and now you've taught him in fifteen minutes. I'm very impressed."

"Thanks, Max, but he's a natural. I only made it fun."

"If we can only keep him interested long enough, I think he'll make a really fine rider one day," Max said.

"Oh brother," Carole mouthed quietly to herself. She rolled her eyes. If she heard one more person singing Zach's praises, she'd throw up. She returned Sunset to her stall and hurried off to tack up her own horse, desperate to put some distance between herself and the boy wonder.

She led Starlight outside and mounted up. The others were chatting together in a small knot. Unfortunately she had to pass by them on her way to the practice ring.

"Hi, Carole. Going for a ride?" Stevie asked.

Before she could answer, Lisa spoke up. "You should have seen how fast Zach picked up on his turns."

"It wasn't as hard as I thought after all," Zach said, grinning happily. "Are there any other games we can play on horseback?"

"Oh sure," Stevie assured him. "Lots."

"I think I'll try a round of jumps," Carole told them. "Keep up the good work, Zach," she added, not wanting them to think she was jealous. *I'm not jealous, of course. Not jealous at all. I'm simply concerned that all this praise will go to Zach's head.*

Carole entered the ring and forced herself to focus. After jogging Starlight around the arena a few times to warm him up, she felt he was ready and set her sights on the first jump. She could tell from his pricked ears that he, too, was eager and paying attention.

With a little pressure from her legs, Carole sent Starlight into a controlled canter. They arrived at the fence in perfect position for the jump. Up and over they soared in absolute unison. With every fence they cleared, Carole felt better and better. At the end of the round they hadn't so much as brushed a pole, let alone knocked one down.

Gleefully she trotted Starlight over to her friends.

"What did you think, guys, not bad, huh?"

"Oh, sorry, Carole," Lisa said. "I was watching Zach. Did it go well?"

Carole was miffed. "I thought so, didn't you, Stevie?"

Stevie shrugged apologetically. "Sorry, I was watching Zach, too."

Carole could hardly believe it. She had just ridden a perfect round of jumps, her timing and style flawless. If this had been a horse show she would have won first place for sure, and absolutely no one had paid her the slightest bit of attention. She felt herself burning inside, and she started to ride away.

"Hey, you want to meet at TD's later?" Stevie called. Tastee Delight was the local ice cream parlor and one of their favorite places for having Saddle Club meetings. Carole opened her mouth to accept when Lisa jumped in.

"Good idea, Stevie. We could take Zach. He looks like he could use a break."

That's it! Carole thought. *If Zach is going, there is no way I am!* "Can't make it, guys," she told them. "I've got work." She headed quickly into the stable.

Actually she didn't have anything planned for the rest of the day at all, but *whatever* she did or *wherever* she went, she did not want to hear another word about Zachary Simpson!

THE EVENING BEFORE the schooling show, The Saddle
Club met at Pine Hollow to make sure everything was
in order.

"I'm glad the other clubs are coming here instead of
us going to them," Lisa said.

"It does make it a lot easier," Carole agreed.
"When we travel to a show it seems like we have to
bring practically every piece of equipment in
the stable."

Stevie smiled happily. "This time if we forget something, all we have to do is run back in here and get it.
Or if something breaks, we've got plenty of replace-
ments right on hand."

"Which reminds me, I need to take one last look at

my tack to make sure none of the straps are worn," Carole said.

"Me too," Lisa agreed.

While Carole and Lisa made a quick but thorough inspection of their equipment, Stevie gave Barq's saddle a once-over, too, since she knew Zach would be riding him in the show. She was surprised by what she found. "Take a look at this," she said, motioning her friends over.

While the leather was in good condition, due to all the years of loving care that Max and his riders devoted to its upkeep, there were obvious flecks of dirt that recent riding had deposited on it.

"It seems Zach forgot to clean his saddle after his last ride," Carole observed.

Lisa held up another piece of equipment. "Not to mention his bridle."

Stevie was amazed. "How could he possibly forget to clean his tack the night before a show?"

"Maybe he's a little scattered," Lisa suggested. "He does have a lot to remember."

Stevie frowned. "Taking care of your equipment is simple, basic horsemanship."

Carole's lips were pressed in a disapproving line. "I know that and you know that, but apparently Zachary Simpson doesn't know that."

Stevie examined a strap with white crusty sweat marks. "He's definitely going to lose points when the judges spot this."

Lisa nodded. "And they *will* spot it."

"Guaranteed, since one of the judges is Max," Carole agreed.

"Okay." Stevie sighed. "We'd better get to work."

Carole put her hands on her hips. "Are we going to do what I think we're going to do?"

Stevie was already reaching for the saddle soap. "Yep."

"I'll get some water," Lisa volunteered.

Carole got the buffing cloths and metal polish from a shelf. "You know, he really should be doing this himself."

Stevie settled herself comfortably and set to work. "I think we should cut him some slack. He is new."

Lisa returned with a bucket of water and placed it where all three of them could reach it easily. "He's really nice. I don't mind helping him out."

Carole started cleaning the snaffle bit. "It's not the helping him out part that bothers me. How is he going to learn if he doesn't bother to study?"

Lisa frowned as she worked on Barq's throatlatch. "He seems enthusiastic about riding, and he's definitely got natural talent."

"Talent without discipline," Carole noted.

From out of nowhere Max's mother, whom everyone called Mrs. Reg, appeared in the doorway. "Working the late shift, girls? I would have thought the three of you would have had your tack ready for the show by now."

"Oh, it's not ours, Mrs. Reg," Lisa told her. "We're helping out a friend."

The elderly lady nodded. "Very commendable. Not everyone enjoys that kind of work."

"But they still need to do it," Carole mumbled.

"Did I ever tell you girls about Sprinkles?"

Stevie shared an *uh-oh* look with her friends. Mrs. Reg was known for her love of telling rambling stories. Her tales usually had hidden meaning, although most of the time the girls couldn't figure out what it was until long after the telling. They had learned that the best thing to do was to simply listen politely.

Mrs. Reg leaned against the door frame, her eyes taking on a faraway look. "Sprinkles was a darling little pony. He was black with little white dots on his muzzle and rump. It made him look like he had been sprinkled with powdered sugar. That's how he got his name, of course."

Stevie nodded. "He sounds cute."

Mrs. Reg continued as though Stevie hadn't spoken. "Sprinkles was an unusual creature, though. He had the smoothest walk of any horse I've ever known. It was almost more of a glide than a walk. He was lovely to watch and a real joy to ride. That made him terrifically useful for beginners to learn on; since there was no jarring, they had no fear of falling off."

"A horse with that smooth of a gait would be very valuable for teaching," Carole observed. "That's an interesting story."

Mrs. Reg looked reproachfully at Carole. "I'm not done yet, dear."

Stevie struggled not to giggle. She had no idea where this story was going, but at least it was passing the time while they worked.

"As I said, his walk was a natural gift, a real talent, and we loved him for it. However, his trot was like sitting on a pogo stick. You know, one of those bouncy things that can shake the fillings out of your teeth?"

The girls nodded.

"His canter was worse. The poor little thing always

gave his best, but there was simply nothing to be done about it."

Max's mother fell quiet for a moment, seemingly lost in her thoughts.

"So I guess you sold him then, huh?" Stevie prompted.

Mrs. Reg looked surprised. "Oh no, dear, not at all." She turned to leave. "Now don't hang around here too late, girls. Tomorrow is a big day." With that, she disappeared down the hallway.

The three girls tried to suppress their laughter until they were sure the older woman was out of earshot, not wanting to hurt her feelings.

"What did that have to do with us?" asked Lisa, snickering softly.

Stevie wiped a tear of choked laughter from her eye. "Where does she get this stuff?"

"And what does it mean?" Carole chuckled.

"Beats me," Stevie admitted. "But Pine Hollow wouldn't be the same without her."

Lisa and Carole agreed.

The girls chatted quietly while they completed their task. By the time they were finished, Barq's saddle and bridle practically gleamed in the dim light of the tack room.

Stevie stretched her cramped back. "I'm going to check on Belle before I head home."

Lisa and Carole accompanied her.

"Any news on her progress?" Lisa asked as they walked to the mare's stall.

"Judy was here yesterday. She says Belle's healing and is well on the way to being completely sound." Stevie had been overjoyed to hear the news. Even though Judy had assured her that Belle's injury wasn't that serious, somewhere in the back of her mind there had been a nagging doubt.

Belle came forward in her stall like a good hostess to greet her visitors. Stevie automatically reached out to stroke her.

"When will you be able to ride her?" Carole asked.

"She'll be ready in another week or so. Which works out fine, because that's when the doctor says I'm allowed to get on her again."

"Excellent!" Lisa said. "We should plan something special for that day."

"Absolutely," Carole agreed. "Trail ride? Picnic?"

Stevie grinned. "How about both? Then TD's and a Saddle Club sleepover! We'll make it a real celebration."

The girls laughed in happy anticipation.

On the way out of the stable, they swung by Sunset's

stall to take a quick look. As usual, the mare was pacing restlessly. Carole called to her and offered her a friendly hand to sniff, but the horse would have none of it.

"Do you think she's okay?" Stevie asked.

Carole shrugged. "I guess so, but her behavior bothers me. I thought she would have settled down by now. She should be feeling more at home after the last couple of weeks, but she seems just as restless as when she arrived."

"Do you think her restlessness means she's getting ready to foal?" Lisa asked.

"Sometimes it does and sometimes it doesn't," Carole answered, moving into the stall.

"Gee, could you vague that up a little?" Stevie cracked.

Carole smiled over her shoulder. "What I mean is that the signs vary from animal to animal. When their time gets near, some horses become restless while others refuse to move at all unless forced to." She brought the mare to a halt.

Stevie watched, intrigued, as Carole examined Sunset more thoroughly. "Are there any absolute signs she's about to go into labor?"

"As a rule, yes," Carole told her. "I'm checking for them now."

Stevie and Lisa fell silent, not wanting to distract their friend. After a few moments Carole seemed satisfied.

"I'm sure she's not ready yet," Carole announced, joining them outside the stall.

Sunset resumed her restless pacing.

"So what *are* the signs?" Lisa asked. Even though all three girls had participated in births before, Carole was the only one who knew all the details about what to look for—and what to expect.

"Walk me to the bus stop and I'll fill you in," Carole offered.

"Are we about to have an 'ick' moment?" Stevie asked.

Carole grinned. "Remember The Saddle Club credo. If you're going to love horses, you have to love *everything* about them."

"Yep, we're going to have an 'ick' moment."

Lisa grimaced. "Come on, Stevie, maybe if we walk fast enough she won't have time to get to the really gross parts."

With that the three girls headed for home at a brisk pace. As far as Stevie was concerned, it wasn't fast enough.

8

IT WAS EARLY morning on the day of the show and most of the participants were still arriving. Since Stevie wasn't competing, she could easily have gotten to Pine Hollow later, but she was eager to spend as much time in Phil Marsten's company as she could.

She watched as Phil carefully unloaded his horse, Teddy, from the rusty but sturdy red-and-white trailer. "Teddy looks like he's in good shape, but I'm not so sure about his rider," she quipped.

Phil smiled good-naturedly. He was used to her sense of humor. In fact, he always said it was one of the things he liked the best about her. "I think I can manage to hold my own."

"That should be good enough, since I won't be riding today."

"As I recall, it was me who snagged the blue ribbon the last time we competed," he reminded her.

"I was having a bad hair day. A girl can't do anything right on a bad hair day."

Phil tied his horse to a rail. "Are you sure you didn't throw yourself off Belle and bump your head in order to avoid the possibility of losing to me again?"

Stevie bristled. She truly adored Phil, but they were both extremely competitive when it came to riding. "Believe me, leaving Belle's saddle was definitely not in my plans," she assured him grimly.

Phil came over and took her hands. "I'm sorry, Stevie. I shouldn't tease you about that. It's bad enough that you got hurt at all, but I don't even like to think about how much worse it could have been."

Stevie was touched to see the concern on his face. He really was the sweetest guy, and the fact that he was horse-crazy made him just about perfect in her eyes. "Don't worry about it. I'll be as good as new in another week. You won't have such an easy time of it at the next show."

Phil released her and went back to work unpacking

his equipment. "You *are* a couple of blue ribbons ahead of me," he acknowledged. "But I intend to cut down your lead today."

"I wouldn't go counting your chickens too soon, Phil," she told him, helping him with his things. "After all, you still have Carole and Lisa to contend with. The other team, Sunny Meadows, also has a couple of good riders."

Phil grinned. "Ah, the key word there is *good*. They have *good* riders, while I consider myself to be a great rider."

Stevie studied his eyes with concern. "Oh my gosh, I think *you* may have a concussion, Phil!"

"Why would you think that?"

"At the rate your head is swelling, what else could it be?"

"Sounds like you two are off to a good start," Carole said, approaching the duo.

"Hi, Carole," Phil greeted her. "I was telling Stevie how I'm going to sweep the blues today."

Carole raised her chin and gave him a challenging look. "In your dreams, Marsten. With me in the competition the best you can hope for today is a few sad seconds."

"Make that thirds," Lisa chimed in as she joined the group.

Phil laughed. "Looks like I'm outnumbered here, but in the ring it's every man for himself."

"Or woman for herself," Lisa countered.

"Speaking of *in the ring*," Carole said, holding up a piece of paper, "I've got the official order for the show."

Everyone crowded around to see if there had had been any changes that they needed to be aware of.

"It looks like they've moved the jumping to later this morning and put a pleasure novice class in its place," Stevie observed.

"Isn't Zach signed up for that one?" Lisa asked.

Stevie nodded. "He sure is." She felt a sudden twinge of guilt. In her excitement to see Phil, she had completely forgotten about Zach. Today was his very first show and he probably needed some help, or at least a little pep talk for the last-minute jitters all riders seem to get before entering the ring. "Has anybody seen him this morning?"

"He was in the stable a few minutes ago," Carole told her.

"How is he?" Stevie asked.

"Cocky," Carole said flatly.

Phil turned to Stevie. "Zach is the new rider you told me about, right?"

"That's him."

"Well, I've got everything ready for my classes," Lisa said. "Why don't we all go over and cheer him on?"

Phil shook his head. "No can do. I still have a lot of things to take care of." He looked fondly at Stevie. "I'll have to meet you later. Okay?"

Stevie smiled at him. They had this whole wonderful day to share together. "No problem," she assured him. "I know how it is. Besides, there's something important I have to tell Zach."

"What's that?" Lisa asked.

"The correct way to accept a ribbon."

Carole looked doubtful. "What makes you so sure he's going to win any?"

"Because none of you is riding in his classes," she replied. "I'll meet you in a couple of minutes."

THE GIRLS FOUND a good spot on the fence from which to view Zach's first class. It was a beginner's pleasure class and Stevie had high expectations. The contestants entered the ring.

"There are only half a dozen competitors including Zach," Lisa observed. "Most of them younger."

"After all we've taught him, this should be cake," Stevie said gleefully.

"You know, age doesn't always denote ability," Carole warned them.

"What are you talking about?" Stevie demanded. "Zach is a natural. Everybody says so. Even Max."

"Yes, I've heard that once or twice," Carole said dryly. "I'm only saying some of those younger riders have been studying a lot longer than Zach. This is his first show, so maybe we shouldn't get our hopes too high."

Lisa nodded. "You're right, of course. He's bound to be nervous and make mistakes. If things go badly, we should really make an effort to support him."

"Agreed," Stevie said. "Who's judging the class, anyway?"

Carole opened her show schedule. "Mr. Baker."

All the girls knew and liked Mr. Baker, who was Phil's riding instructor and the owner of Cross County Stables.

Lisa pointed to the entrance to the ring. "Shhh, they're starting."

Stevie watched the class with excited anticipation. At first everything went fine. Mr. Baker asked for a walk and then an extended walk. Next came a reversal of directions and a move into the trot.

Lisa grabbed Stevie's arm excitedly. "He turned inside on the reversal exactly like we taught him."

Stevie said nothing. She had noticed that Barq's collected trot was faster than the horse's in front of him, which meant he was quickly closing the distance between them. She waited to see what Zach would do about it.

Zach seemed oblivious to the situation. Instead of passing the slower animal on the inside, as was acceptable, he allowed Barq to get closer and closer to the other horse's rump.

"Oh no," Lisa whispered. "Zach's riding up on the back of that other horse."

"Didn't you warn him about that?" Stevie whispered back.

"I most certainly did," Lisa defended herself. "He must have forgotten."

"If he gets any closer he could get kicked," Carole said.

Mr. Baker called for a reversal and a canter. "Whew!" Stevie said with relief. "That should help."

Zach made the change in direction and gait fine,

and as soon as Barq began to canter, a big grin plastered itself across his face.

"Look at him," Stevie laughed. "You sure can't say he doesn't enjoy riding."

Carole shook her head. "Too bad he's on the wrong lead."

"What? Oh no!" Stevie wailed when she saw it was true. "Didn't he listen to you at all?" she demanded of Lisa.

"Me?" Lisa said, looking indignant. "Lead changes were your department, not mine."

Stevie slapped her forehead. "That's right. Didn't he listen to *me* at all?"

"All right, you guys, take it easy," Carole told them. "It's his first class and his first show. I bet he does better as he goes along."

Stevie sure hoped so. "Look, Zach has Barq on the right lead now," she said with relief. "I guess he did listen to me after all."

"He looks nice at the canter," Carole admitted. "Very smooth."

After the riders circled a couple of times around the ring, Mr. Baker called for a walk. All the riders dutifully pulled their mounts down from the canter— all except Zach, who kept right on going around the ring.

"What is he doing?" Lisa asked, shocked. "Isn't he paying attention?"

"Maybe he didn't hear the call," Stevie suggested anxiously.

"You'd think he'd notice everybody else is walking," Carole muttered.

Zach finally slowed Barq to a walk. The incident hadn't lasted long but Stevie feared the damage had been done.

The class ended shortly after that. Mr. Baker called the riders to order and began handing out the ribbons. Stevie watched with a sinking heart as prize after prize was given and none of them went to Zach. Finally his name was called to accept the sixth ribbon. He had placed last in the class.

Stevie was sure Zach would be devastated. "Come on. We'd better go talk to him."

"Let's all try to think of something positive to say," Lisa suggested.

The Saddle Club caught up with Zach as he headed back to the stable. He was frowning and his face was flushed. It was obvious he was angry.

"Sorry, Zach," Stevie said gently. "That didn't go exactly according to plan."

Zach spun to face them. "I can't believe he gave me last place!" he fumed. "Didn't that guy see how good I was at cantering? I was the best one in the ring. He must be totally blind!"

"You did keep going after he called for a walk," Carole reminded him gently.

"I know. I wanted to make sure he saw how good Barq and I were."

Stevie could hardly believe what she was hearing. "Zach, it's a terrible breach of etiquette to ignore the judge's instructions."

"Even if you think you have a good reason to," Lisa added.

"I only wanted to show him that we were the best," Zach grumbled. "That's no reason to give me last place. That old dude obviously doesn't like me."

Carole frowned. "Judging isn't personal, Zach, and I've never heard anyone accuse Mr. Baker of being biased before."

"There's always a first time," he said grimly. "Lots of those other kids made mistakes. It's not like I was the only one."

Stevie was concerned by his attitude. Instead of learning a lesson from the experience, Zach was letting it make him bitter. Apparently he thought losing was anybody's fault but his own. A big mistake. She considered pointing this out but then decided not to; he still had more classes to compete in and she wanted to help him focus on them in a positive manner. "Yes, there were other kids messing up," she said, choosing her words carefully. "Maybe Mr. Baker didn't happen to see them when they did it. He hasn't got eyes in back of his head."

Zach seemed to brighten at that. "Yeah. You're right, Stevie, I didn't think of that. You know what they say: Timing in life is everything. I was unlucky, that's all. You guys wait till the next class. I'm going for gold!"

"Blue," Lisa said.

"Huh?"

"The first-place ribbon is blue," she told him.

Zach smiled. "Whatever. This time it's got my name on it for sure!"

Later in the morning, Stevie, Lisa, Phil, and Zach cheered Carole on from the sidelines as she competed in the jumping class. Watching her friend soar gracefully over the barriers made Stevie itch to get back in the saddle. Not being able to ride was killing her, and, worse, she still had another week to go.

"That looks really fun," Zach said enthusiastically. "I've got to get in on that."

"You can," Lisa assured him. "But you've got to conquer the basics first."

Zach made a face. "I hate all this technical stuff. Seems like a waste of time to me."

"You have to walk before you can run," Stevie reminded him.

Zach grinned. "If you can already run, why bother to walk at all?"

Stevie shook her head and focused on the ring. Carole had done an excellent job, not only going clean but doing it with impeccable style. At the end of the class she was the only one to have completed the course with no faults, which meant that she wouldn't even have to compete in a jump-off. She had won first place hands down.

The group hooted and hollered as Carole graciously accepted her ribbon, then rushed to congratulate her.

"Nice riding, Carole," Phil told her. "I couldn't have done it better myself."

"That's for sure!" Stevie told him with a twinkle in her eye.

"Hey, I've got a dressage class in a few minutes. What about my morale?" he mockingly complained. "You're supposed to be rooting for me!"

Stevie punched him lightly in the shoulder. "Don't be silly, you do enough of that for both of us."

"We'd better get going, Phil," said Lisa, who was riding in the same class. "The event is scheduled to start soon."

As the two of them headed off to get their horses, Stevie returned to her place at the rail, but this time with Carole and Zach beside her.

"So, who are you going to cheer for?" Zach asked.

Stevie was torn. "My boyfriend and one of my very best friends in the world going head to head . . . Hmmm . . . I think I'll hope for the best for both of them and be grateful I'm not in Max's shoes today."

"If it's close, I bet Max will favor Lisa," Zach said. "Must be nice having your own instructor be the judge."

"Zach!" Carole cried indignantly. "Max would never be biased toward any rider."

Zach had the good grace to look sheepish. "Sorry, C. You're right. Max is a righteous dude."

They all settled down to watch the competition. Zach stayed long enough to watch both Phil and Lisa compete, but Stevie noticed he looked bored and restless. After a while he wandered away, telling the two girls he had to get ready for his next class.

As it turned out, Phil took the blue ribbon and Lisa

snagged a close second place. Stevie and Carole hurried over to them.

"First place, huh?" Stevie said, admiring Phil's ribbon. "I'll probably be hearing about this for the next few weeks. Of course it goes without saying that if I had been in the class, this ribbon would be mine."

Phil laughed. "If it goes without saying then why are you saying it?"

"Just making sure we all know where we stand," Stevie said loftily. She turned to Lisa, who was gazing happily at her red second-place ribbon. "Good job, Lisa."

Lisa beamed. "Thanks, Stevie. Hey, where's Zach?"

"He's got another class in a few minutes," Carole told her. "Let's go watch. Maybe he's got himself together now."

Stevie settled into her place next to Phil, keeping her fingers crossed that things would go better for Zach this time.

This was a simple pleasure class. The idea was when the bell sounded once, the riders were to change to the next fastest gait; when the bell rang twice, back to the next slower one.

As usual they all started at a walk. Right from

the beginning things went wrong. Zach's riding technique was fine—in fact, Stevie thought it was better than ever—but he kept getting confused about which gait he should be in. He was clearly having trouble remembering what the bells meant, and unfortunately it was causing chaos among the other riders.

Stevie groaned as Zach missed yet another cue. "This is terrible," she said, clutching Phil's arm tightly. "I can hardly stand to watch."

"I thought you said this guy was a phenomenal rider," Phil said doubtfully.

"He is," Lisa said. "At least he seems to be when he's not competing."

"If he doesn't start concentrating, Mrs. Schoef is going to dismiss him," Carole noted.

A few more minutes passed with Zach showing no improvement, and Carole's prediction came true. The judge disqualified him and asked him to leave the ring.

Stevie could tell even from where she was watching that Zach was hugely upset. At first he pulled Barq to a stop and stared at the judge as if he couldn't believe his ears. Then, instead of walking his horse quietly out of the ring, he kicked Barq into a gallop and raced angrily to exit at the other side of the arena. He pulled up just short of the gate and flung himself out of the saddle, using the same technique he had shown off at the gymkhana.

Phil looked impressed. "Maybe this guy can ride after all."

Stevie frowned. "Rider or not, there's no excuse for that kind of behavior. His tantrum is a bad reflection on all the Horse Wise riders!" *Especially The Saddle Club*, she added in her mind, *because everyone knows we've been coaching him.*

Angrily she and the others went to find Zach.

To everyone's amazement and dismay, all they found was Barq, abandoned and cropping grass near the out gate, with his reins trailing on the ground. Zach was nowhere to be seen.

"I can't believe Zach would leave Barq here without even tying him up," Stevie said with disappointment.

Lisa approached the horse. "That was totally outrageous. Barq could easily have hurt himself if he'd stepped on these loose reins." She gathered up the dangling straps.

"He's lucky his horse didn't run away," Carole said. "Most animals would have, especially with all this activity going on around them."

Stevie was appalled. Had Zach learned nothing

about his responsibilities as a rider over the last few weeks? He had put Barq in a dangerous situation and only thought of himself. "Come on. First things first, let's put poor Barq away. Then later on I suggest we have a serious talk with one Zachary Simpson."

9

THE SADDLE CLUB dutifully removed Barq's tack and made sure he had food and water before leaving him in his stall.

Carole sighed. "I guess it's a safe bet Zach won't be wanting to ride anymore today."

"I still can't believe he would leave Barq alone like that," Lisa said, shaking her head. "You'd think he didn't care about him at all."

Carole was still struggling to understand it herself. "Why would he do something so irresponsible?"

Stevie laughed harshly. "He's a boy, that's why. My brothers are always doing dumb stuff they know they're not supposed to do, and they always have the same excuse: 'I forgot.'"

An idea started to form in Carole's mind but she couldn't quite lock on to it.

"Hey, Carole, don't you have another class soon?" Lisa reminded her.

Carole checked her watch. "Yikes! The hunter seat. I've got to go!"

Stevie frowned. "I was going to try to find Zach, but I'd definitely rather watch you."

"What about me?" Lisa demanded. "I'm competing in the serpentine right before lunch. Don't I count?"

"You know I wouldn't miss it," Stevie laughed. Then she grew more serious. "After all the work we put into that, someone might as well benefit."

Carole led the way to Starlight's stall to make a final check of her equipment. When she was satisfied, she pulled herself into the saddle and touched the horseshoe for luck. She was about to ride over to the ring when a thought occurred to her. "Stevie, don't go looking for Zach," she advised. "He's probably not feeling too good about himself right now. We might only make things worse if we talk to him before he calms down."

Stevie looked unconvinced. "Somebody needs to tell him he can't act like that in a show."

"Maybe that should come from Max," Lisa suggested. "He is the instructor. Besides, Carole and I need a cheerleader for our classes and we've elected you."

"All right," Stevie agreed. "Anyway, this is too nice a day to let Zach's temper tantrum ruin it."

Carole made her way to the in gate, joining a small knot of waiting riders.

The hunter seat class consisted of a set of jumps in a figure eight. The obstacles were smaller than the ones Carole had competed over earlier, but this time she was going to have to jump them without the use of her stirrups. Points would be awarded to whoever best maintained the correct style.

Carole pushed the problems with Zach out of her mind and concentrated on the work at hand.

The first part of the course came easy, but halfway through her ride Starlight gave one of the rails a hard knock. Carole's heart skipped a beat as she waited for it to fall, but she heard nothing and the crowd didn't react, so she figured she'd gotten lucky. Unfortunately, the jolt had rocked her slightly out of position, and although she was quick to correct it, she knew she had probably lost a few points.

A few more jumps and her turn was complete. Overall Carole felt she had done pretty well, and when she heard Lisa and Stevie whooping at her from the sidelines, she was sure of it. Her spirits soared.

At the end of the class, Carole was pleased to accept

her red ribbon for second place. She quickly tied up Starlight and rushed to join Stevie and Phil in time to catch Lisa in the serpentine class.

"How do you think she'll do?" Phil asked.

"Hard to say," Carole answered. "You know how tricky flying lead changes can be."

Phil grunted his acknowledgment.

"I worked with her and Zach on them," Stevie told them. "Lisa thought she needed the work, but she looked really good in practice."

"It doesn't matter if she wins," said Phil, "as long as she does her best."

Stevie looked at him with affection. That sort of attitude was exactly why she liked him so much.

"Is Zach going to ride in this event like he planned?" Phil asked.

"Not likely." Stevie snorted. "What a waste of my time that turned out to be."

Carole was saddened to hear Stevie say that. She was about to say something when Lisa's name was called and all thoughts of Zach were pushed from her mind.

Lisa did very well in the class. She wasn't the fastest through the course, but she managed to keep her lead changes consistent and correct. In the end she was rewarded with a third-place ribbon. The only downside was that snotty Veronica diAngelo had taken first.

The gang hooted and hollered their approval as they watched Lisa accept her prize, then went to meet her.

"Good job, Lisa!" cried Stevie.

"Most excellent," Carole said, giving her a hug.

The girl beamed happily. "Thanks, guys, but I'm sure glad that's over with!"

"Of course you are," crowed Veronica, who was passing by. "After all, no one wants to revel in their failures." She caressed the blue ribbon on Danny's bridle meaningfully.

"Look Veronica—" started Carole, but she was interrupted by a loud gong. Mrs. Reg was calling everyone to the main house for a barbecue. Carole bit her tongue. "Come on, guys, that's lunch."

Veronica waved a hand at their group as though shooing them away. "I wouldn't want to keep you from the trough," she sneered; and with an obnoxious laugh and a flip of her long, glossy black hair, she moved off into the crowd of riders and horses.

Stevie glared at her. "I suppose that's her way of saying she won't be staying for lunch."

"I, for one, hope it is," Phil said, putting a comforting hand on Stevie's shoulder. "I don't know about the rest of you, but she sure puts me off my feed."

"Don't you think we should go and see if we can help out?" Lisa suggested.

"Good idea," Stevie agreed. "We've got a lot of hungry riders to feed around here."

"I'll pitch in, too," Phil offered.

"Negative," Stevie told him firmly. "You're our guest today. Go hang out with your friends until we're ready to serve, then we'll join you."

Phil shrugged. "Okay, see you at lunch!" He quickly headed off.

Stevie crossed her arms on her chest. "Can you believe that?" she said indignantly. "He didn't even try to insist."

Lisa shook her head resignedly. "Avoiding work. It's got to be a boy thing."

That did it. Carole had a sudden insight into what was going on with Zachary Simpson. She wanted to share her revelation with the others, but it would have to wait. Right now, The Saddle Club was urgently needed to play host to the other Pony Clubs, and there was no way they could get out of it like Phil just had.

AFTER ALL THE guest riders had departed and most of the chores were finished, the three girls slipped up to the hayloft to talk over the events of the day.

"I'm exhausted," Stevie declared, throwing herself down on a convenient hay bale.

"You can say that again," Lisa agreed from where she, too, had collapsed.

Carole stretched her stiff back and wriggled her tired toes. "Do you think Mrs. Reg saw us come up here?"

"I don't think so," Stevie said. "Besides, it's not like we haven't earned a break. I've never washed so many dishes in my life. Not to mention set tables, carried food . . ."

Lisa took over. "Peeled vegetables, grated cheese, poured drinks . . ."

"Swept up, emptied the trash, cleaned out the barbecue pit . . . ," Carole added.

For a moment the three of them were silent.

"What a great day!" Stevie burst out with a wide grin.

"The best," Carole laughed.

"I love days like this," Lisa declared happily.

The Saddle Club looked at each other contentedly.

"The only bad thing about today was that I won't be able to see Phil again for a while," Stevie sighed wistfully. "I wish he didn't live so far away."

Lisa frowned. "Actually that wasn't the only bad thing about today. Zach didn't exactly hold up well under pressure."

"He made us look like bad teachers," Stevie said, starting to fume. "I don't think he used anything we taught him over the last two weeks."

"In one ear and out the other," Lisa agreed. "We gave him all that time and attention so that he could do well in his first show, and what does he do? He runs off in a snit without even taking care of his horse!"

"He acted like a rank amateur," Stevie declared.

"A jerk!" exclaimed Lisa.

Carole listened to her friends without saying anything. She understood they were severely disappointed and needed to let their frustrations out. After a bit more grousing, however, she decided to speak up. "Actually, I think I know exactly what his problem is."

They both stopped talking and stared at her.

"You do?" Lisa asked.

Carole nodded.

"So tell," Stevie demanded.

Carole shrugged. "He acted like a typical boy."

"He is a boy!" Stevie cried. "That's no excuse!"

"You're right," Carole said. "It's not an excuse but it is an explanation."

Her friends looked puzzled.

Carole squirmed on her hay bale. "First, I think you should know . . ." She sighed. "I've been a little jealous of Zach and all the attention he's been getting around here. It seemed like even you two wanted to spend more time with *him* than me."

Lisa looked stricken. "We didn't know you felt like that."

"We just thought Zach needed some help. We didn't mean to cut you out," Stevie told her.

Carole smiled. "You didn't cut me out. I cut myself out. The truth is, you guys invited me to help all along. I didn't want to because . . . like I said, I was jealous. But that's over now and I'm determined to make it up to Zach."

Stevie groaned and flopped back on the hay bale. "Take it from Lisa and me, Carole, he's not worth the bother."

"I hate to say it, but I agree with Stevie," Lisa said, shaking her head. "All that boy is interested in is galloping around like a madman. He can't keep his mind on an instruction for more than five minutes."

"He *still* had his elbows and heels sticking out in the show today," Stevie pointed out. "Lisa and I must have told him about that a million times!"

"*Two* million," Lisa declared. "He's got no discipline and no focus."

"And he doesn't seem to be interested in getting any," Stevie finished.

"Don't you see?" Carole said. "That's our problem, not his."

Her two friends looked at her like she was crazy.

"What?" Stevie cried.

"How is that *our* problem?" Lisa demanded.

"It's our problem that we can't accept him for who he is. Studying isn't his thing—"

"But Carole," Lisa interrupted, "if he doesn't study, he's never going to win a ribbon in any show!"

Carole nodded. "That's probably true."

"Then what's the point of riding at all?" Stevie demanded.

"That's the point for you and Lisa and me. We enjoy riding in shows. We enjoy the discipline. We like competing against other people, so we can see where we are in our skills and how much further there is to go," she said passionately. "That's what *we* love about riding, but that's not what *Zach* loves about it."

Lisa frowned. "You mean he just loves riding?"

"Yes, exactly!" Carole cried, pleased that her friends were starting to get her point. "Think about it. Competition is always a huge amount of pressure. Even for people who enjoy it."

"You're saying Zach can't handle it?" Stevie asked.

"Maybe he's just not interested right now," Lisa said thoughtfully.

"Maybe he never will be," Carole pointed out.

"Well, he doesn't seem to love horses as much as we do, either," Stevie said.

Carole shook her head. "I don't think that's true. I think Zach gets something different out of riding than we do. He clearly loves it—you only have to look at his face whenever he's galloping around to see that."

"I have to admit I've never seen anyone look happier to be on a horse," Lisa said. "Not even one of us."

"I think Zach simply wants to ride and be buddies with his horse. That's what brings him pleasure."

"I still think he'd like jumping if he tried it," Stevie declared.

Carole nodded. "I think he would too, but that's something that requires a lot of training and discipline."

"Maybe if he saw us do it often enough, he'd realize that good riding form—elbows in, heels down, et cetera—makes it easier to ride fast, the way he likes it. It's safer, too. It would inspire him to try to learn," Lisa suggested.

"But to see it, he would have to be around the stables a lot," Stevie said.

Lisa shrugged. "So?"

Stevie rubbed her forehead like she had a sudden headache. "That could be a problem."

Carole frowned. "Why would that a problem?"

Stevie sighed. "I was going to tell you this as soon as I heard, but then I got caught up in all the chores and saying good-bye to Phil. I guess I forgot."

Carole and Lisa looked at her expectantly.

"Zach's not coming back."

"What?" Carole cried. "Did he tell you that?"

Stevie shook her head. "Max did. He told me while we were cleaning out the charcoal pit."

Lisa looked dismayed. "What exactly did he say?"

Stevie shrugged. "Max said Zach told him he not only doesn't want to compete in another show, but he never wants to ride a horse again in his life!"

Carole and Lisa exchanged shocked looks.

"But Zach loves riding!" Carole cried.

"Do you think maybe we had something to do with his quitting?" Lisa asked, looking guilty.

"We did push him pretty hard," Stevie admitted.

Carole shook her head with dismay. This was terrible. "I can't believe The Saddle Club may have been responsible for driving someone away from riding," she moaned. "We have to do something. We have to get Zach back in the saddle."

"But how?" Stevie asked. "If he doesn't want to ride, we can't force him."

"Maybe," Carole admitted, "but we have to try."

"Is this going to be a Saddle Club project?" Lisa asked.

Carole nodded. "You bet! I don't know how we're going to do it, but Zach Simpson is going to ride again!"

THE SADDLE CLUB had agreed to pay Zach a visit, and since Lisa knew where he lived, she was leading the way.

"Are you sure about this?" Carole asked.

"Of course," Lisa assured her. "His house is across the meadow from Pine Hollow. If we cut through these woods, we'll make it there in almost half the time."

"I wasn't talking about the shortcut," Carole told her. "I mean are you two sure this direct approach is the best way to handle him?"

Stevie shrugged. "All I know is that our chances of convincing Zach to come back to riding are better if we can talk to him face to face."

"But if Max couldn't get him to change his mind, I don't see how we're going to," Carole said glumly.

"Look, we have to start somewhere, don't we?" Stevie picked her way around a bush. "I didn't exactly hear anybody else coming up with a brilliant plan."

"True," Carole admitted. "This would be so much easier if we understood boys better. Maybe then we'd be able to figure out how to handle this."

"Don't worry so much," Stevie said. "If Plan A fails, we'll go with Plan B."

"I didn't know you had a Plan B," Lisa said.

"What is it?" Carole asked.

"Let's just say I guarantee that Zach will return to Pine Hollow at least one more time," Stevie told them smugly.

"Look." Carole pointed. "Is that his house?"

Lisa nodded. "That's it."

Since the girls had cut across the fields instead of taking the street route, they found themselves approaching Zach's home from the backyard. It was a neat, white, two-story house with green shutters. The entire property was surrounded by a double-railed white fence—high enough to keep most large stray animals out, but not three determined members of The Saddle Club.

Stevie was the first to clamber over, followed quickly by Carole and Lisa.

"Should we knock on the back door?" Lisa asked doubtfully.

Carole shook her head. "I think it would look a little strange to Zach's parents if we suddenly showed up in their backyard."

"Especially since they don't know us," Stevie agreed. "Let's head to the front." The three of them quietly made their way around the house. Stevie was about to knock when Lisa grabbed her hand.

"Wait! What exactly are we going to say to him? 'We're sorry that you're too immature to learn to ride correctly'?"

Stevie rolled her eyes. "Oh yeah, Lisa, that would definitely score big points."

"Maybe you'd better let Stevie and me do the talking," Carole told her.

Lisa nodded.

Stevie took a big breath and rapped smartly on the door. The truth was, she had no idea what she was going to say. The Saddle Club was flying by the seat of their riding britches on this one.

They only had to wait a few moments before the door was opened by a middle-aged lady. She had white-blond hair and green eyes exactly like Zach's, so Stevie figured she was his mother.

"Good afternoon, Mrs. Simpson," she began politely. "We're friends of Zach's from Pine Hollow. I'm Stevie, and this is Lisa and Carole."

Mrs. Simpson smiled and glanced backward over her shoulder.

From where Stevie was standing she could see a staircase, but she couldn't tell if anyone was on it.

"How nice to meet you, girls," Mrs. Simpson said. "It's good to know Zach is making friends."

"Oh, he is, Mrs. Simpson," Carole assured her. "Everybody likes Zach."

Considering that Carole had only recently confessed to being terribly jealous of the boy, Stevie struggled to suppress a guffaw.

"He kind of crashed and burned at the show this morning," Lisa blurted out. "Do you think we could see him?"

Stevie could barely keep herself from kicking Lisa in the shin. If Zach was listening, and she suspected he was, that little comment wouldn't help their cause.

"What she means is," Carole said, rushing in, "that almost everyone has problems at their first show, and we wanted to make sure that Zach understood that and wasn't feeling bad."

"So Zach wasn't the only one who had trouble?" Mrs. Simpson asked. Her eyes darted quickly over her shoulder again. "There were other kids who had problems?"

"Oh, tons," Stevie exaggerated. "Lots of people made major mistakes, but since Zach left early, he didn't get to see them." If the guy was listening, Stevie hoped she was getting through to him.

"So, would it be possible for us see him, Mrs. Simpson?" Lisa ventured again.

There was another quick glance at the staircase. Then Mrs. Simpson shook her head regretfully. "I'm sorry, girls, Zach . . . isn't available right now."

Stevie was disappointed. "Do you think he'll be coming by the stables later this week?" she asked hopefully.

Mrs. Simpson looked a little sad. "I don't know exactly what Zach's riding plans are right now. Don't you all go to the same school?"

"Stevie doesn't," Lisa said, "but Carole and I do. Zach and I have a class together."

"Maybe you could talk to him then," Mrs. Simpson suggested. "Sometimes boys just need a little space, don't they, girls?" She gave a conspiritorial wink.

It was obvious to Stevie that they were going to

have to try a different plan. "We understand, Mrs. Simpson. Would you please tell Zach we stopped by?"

"Of course, dear, and it was very nice to meet you all."

The girls said their farewells and moved reluctantly toward the sidewalk.

As soon as Stevie heard the door close behind them, she changed direction. "Come on, guys! Backyard!" She quickly led the way around the house.

Lisa grinned. "Plan B?"

"Plan B," Stevie confirmed. She spotted a few pebbles on the ground and scooped them up. "Which window do you think is his?"

Lisa pointed. "Try that one."

Stevie pitched one of the pebbles and it pinged against the window.

"Stevie, no!" Carole squealed. "You could break the glass."

"No chance," Stevie said, throwing another stone. "They do this in the movies all the time."

Although the first pebble seemed to get no reaction, Stevie was almost certain that the curtain twitched a little after the second one hit. "Zach!" she called. "We know you're there. Why don't you come down and talk to us?"

The girls waited.

After a moment Stevie tried again. "Come on, Zach," she coaxed. "Aren't we still friends?" She was almost positive she could see a shadowy figure behind the half-drawn curtains. She decided to take another approach. "Hey, did you know you left your math book in your cubby at Pine Hollow?"

Nothing.

"Sooner or later you're going to have to come get it!"

Suddenly a hand reached out and abruptly pulled the window shade down.

Lisa sighed. "So much for Plan B."

"That was it?" Carole asked incredulously. "*That* was Plan B?"

Stevie shrugged. "Sorry." Her two friends were giving her annoyed looks. "Hey, he did leave his math book and he is going to have to get it."

"What good does that do us?" Lisa demanded. "We can't exactly stake out his cubby day and night."

"What if he goes to get it early before school?" Carole asked. "What if he sends his mom to get it for him?"

"I didn't say it was a flawless plan," Stevie said, sulking. "That's why it was only Plan B."

"More like Plan L for Lousy if you ask me," Lisa muttered.

Stevie frowned. "Well, we'd better come up with a new one fast or this is one Saddle Club project that's going to fail."

Carole headed for the fence. "Come on, you two. I want to check on Sunset before the sleepover at Lisa's."

Carole climbed over the rail with a scowling Stevie and a gloomy Lisa trailing behind. The girls were silent most of the way back to the stable, each one of them trying desperately to come up with a way to get through to Zach. By the time they reached Pine Hollow, they were almost ready to admit defeat.

Stevie made a beeline for Belle's stall. Her horse's leg was no longer bandaged, so it was easy to check for heat and swelling. Everything looked fine. Stevie fished in her pocket for a piece of carrot. "You're doing great," she told the mare as she fed her. "I can't wait to get back in the saddle." She left Belle with an affectionate tug on her forelock. As she passed through the stable she saw Lisa leaving Prancer's stall. "Do you want any carrot? I have some left."

Lisa smiled. "Thanks, but I brought some, too. Maybe Carole would like a bit."

They found Carole in Starlight's stall, talking softly to the animal as she patted him.

Stevie waved a piece of carrot at her. "Hey, Carole, you want any?"

Carole shook her head. "You know I don't believe in too many treats."

"Glad you're not *my* mother," Lisa teased her.

"Maybe Sunset would like some," Stevie said innocently.

Carole took the bait. "Absolutely not!" she said, wagging a finger at Stevie. "You know Sunset is on a very strict diet."

Stevie laughed. "Got ya."

Carole laughed, too. "Okay," she admitted. "Maybe I am going overboard. How much damage can one piece of carrot do?"

"Come on, let's feed it to her and get over to my house," Lisa said. "I'm hungry and tired."

The girls peeked into Sunset's stall. To their surprise, instead of her usual incessant pacing, the mare was standing in a corner, shifting her weight from side to side.

The girls entered the stall and approached her.

"Is she okay?" Lisa asked.

"Looks all right to me," Stevie offered.

Carole was frowning. "Why is she doing that?"

"You tell us," Lisa said. "You're the expert around here."

Carole shook her head. "There's so much I don't know."

"She doesn't seem to be distressed," Lisa observed. "I bet she's fine."

"Maybe her feet are hurting from the extra weight she's carrying," Stevie said. "I know mine would be."

"I'm going to phone Judy," Carole declared, leaving the stall.

"She's okay, Carole," Stevie called after her. "You're overreacting."

Carole didn't stop. "It'll only take a minute."

Stevie sighed and found a place to sit down. "She's got that worrywart thing down pretty good," she said to Lisa.

"She might be right, though," Lisa said, plunking down next to her. "I mean, better safe than sorry, right?"

"I guess," Stevie replied. She yawned and stretched. It had been a busy and emotional day, and she was starting to feel the effects of it.

Carole was back a few minutes later.

Stevie got up. "What did she say?"

"She says she doesn't think there's anything to worry about." Carole reentered Sunset's stall. "She's going to stop by in the morning to make sure."

"Great. Now can we head to my house?" Lisa asked.

"I second that idea," Stevie said enthusiastically.

"Let me take one last look," Carole begged, moving around the horse.

Stevie was getting impatient. "Come on, Carole, Judy said Sunset is fine. Give it a rest!"

"All right, all right," Carole conceded, reluctantly leaving the stall. "I guess I'm being a worrywart."

Stevie slipped an arm around her and pointed her toward the exit. "You? A worrywart? Never!"

CAROLE ROLLED OVER, buried her face in her pillow, and snuggled deeper into the warmth of her covers. She wasn't exactly sure what had awakened her, but she was determined to go back to sleep. The sky was only just starting to lighten with the first hint of dawn, and there were still hours of wonderful horsey dreams to dream.

Two minutes later she was still tossing and turning. Something felt wrong. There was a reason she had woken up. A dream. No, *more* than a dream. A premonition. Her mind was still fuzzy with sleep and she couldn't quite recall the fleeting images, but she sensed that it was important. It had something to do with horses . . . and stables . . . and . . .

All at once it came to her in a rush, causing her to

sit straight up. Sunset's stall door. She couldn't remember bolting it when she left last night!

Surely I must have, she reasoned. *After all these years of riding, it would be a habit by now. Wouldn't it?* Suddenly she felt a wave of doubt. Trying to stay calm, she went over what she remembered of last night's events. Checking Sunset one last time. Stevie and Lisa urging her to hurry up. Leaving the stall. Leaving Pine Hollow on their way to Lisa's for the sleepover. All of those things were crystal clear in her head, but nowhere was there a memory of actually latching the mare's door.

Carole's imagination was suddenly flooded with visions of all the trouble Sunset could get into. She knew from having watched the mare over the last few weeks how feisty and curious she was. Carole's stomach clenched. What if she got into the feed room and started eating the molasses that was kept there for mixing with the oats? She might not have the good sense to stop before she made herself sick. She might get colic. What would that do to her foal at this late stage of her pregnancy? Carole's heart started thumping with anxiety. Worse yet, Sunset might wander outside into the yard. With no one watching out for her, there were hundreds of ways for her to get hurt. She might even be able to get out of the main gate and into the street!

Carole looked over at Lisa and Stevie. They were both sound asleep. She considered waking them but then remembered how they had all been so wiped out the night before. In fact, they had been so exhausted from the day's activities that they had even skipped the hours of horse chat that were a Saddle Club tradition at sleepovers and had gone straight to bed. No, this was her problem and she was going to take care of it herself.

She slipped out from under the covers, found her clothes, and put them on as quietly as possible. Then she scribbled a quick note telling her friends where she was going. After all, they would think it strange if they woke up and found her gone; she certainly didn't want to alarm anyone unnecessarily.

Carrying her boots, Carole let herself out of the room and tiptoed downstairs. A glance at her watch told her it was five o'clock. Good. Even if the Atwoods were early risers, they still wouldn't be up at this time of the morning. Maybe if she were quick she could make it to Pine Hollow and back before anyone missed her. That way no one would even have to know about this embarrassing lapse of responsibility.

Once outside the house she stopped only long enough to pull on her boots, then she hurried toward the stables. Luckily it wasn't far and she would be there soon. Soon, however didn't seem soon enough to her.

All the way there, her mind was filled with visions of the different kinds of catastrophes Sunset might have gotten into because of her carelessness.

Sweating and out of breath, Carole ran to the barn, looking around the area anxiously. Everything appeared normal—peaceful and serene in the early-morning light. She hurriedly slipped inside, shutting the big door tightly her behind.

As her eyes adjusted to the dim light she sighed with relief. There was no sign of trouble. She gave a little laugh. She'd been terrified that she would find Sunset wreaking havoc in Mrs. Reg's office: desk turned over, papers scattered everywhere, the phone off its hook beep-beep-beeping. . . . But all was calm and quiet, as usual. So far, so good.

The heads of a few sleepy horses poked over their half doors as Carole hurried toward the foaling stall. *I'm probably just being a worrywart like Stevie says*, Carole told herself, *but this will only take a couple of minutes and then I'll be back at Lisa's and tucked in bed, snug and warm.*

It was dark in the corner where Sunset's stall was located, and although she couldn't make out anything of the interior, a huge rush of relief swept over her when she saw that the bottom half of the door was closed.

She went to peek in on the mare when, to her utter horror, she saw the latch wasn't locked at all. Carole yanked open the stall and she felt her heart drop all the way into her boots. It was empty! Sunset was gone!

In a panic, Carole rushed outside to check the paddock. There was no sign of the horse—she had obviously nudged the door open and taken off, and the door had swung closed behind her.

Carole forced herself to calm down. Sunset had to be somewhere. She obviously hadn't gotten out through the front door, so maybe she had wandered out the back and into the schooling ring. With any luck she would still be there.

Carole hurried to the ring. No horse. She raced through the first ring into a second, where it opened into a large field behind the stable.

With her heart pounding in her ears, Carole checked the final gate. It was unlatched! It was possible the mare could have figured out how to open it herself, but Carole suspected that one of the many inexperienced riders who had been roaming around the day before was the real culprit. She ran back to the stable. Who it was didn't matter. That field was big and Sunset could be anywhere.

Carole quickly grabbed Starlight's tack and rushed

136

to saddle him up. "Sorry, boy, no time for a grooming this morning," she told him as she worked.

Horse and rider were ready to go in record time and she leaped into the saddle, urging Starlight into action. They had to find Sunset!

CAROLE PUSHED STARLIGHT into a canter as soon as she got to the field. Since she had no idea which way Sunset might have gone, she intended to cover as much territory as quickly as possible.

Every minute that passed without a sign of the mare seemed like twenty. She kept Starlight at a steady pace, scanning all around her as she rode. Frequently she rose high in her stirrups so that she could see even farther. The beautiful trees and bushes that she had always loved to ride through now seemed like the enemy, blocking her view and possibly hiding Sunset from her.

Finally Carole pulled to a halt. "I never knew this field was so big," she said to her horse. "Where could she be?"

138

Suddenly Starlight pricked his ears and let out a whinny. Carole's heart leaped. Maybe Starlight was reacting to the smell of the mare. *If I give him his head he might take me right to her*, she thought.

Sure enough, as soon as she released contact with his mouth, Starlight headed off at a brisk walk. His ears were pricked far forward and every now and then he let out another whinny. As they cleared the last of a small knot of trees, Carole heard grunting. Seconds later she spotted Sunset.

Her mouth went dry with terror. The mare was lying down groaning. She had gone into labor!

She quickly dismounted and tied Starlight to a tree to keep him out of the way. This was one time Sunset was going to have to accept her company whether she wanted to or not.

As Carole quietly approached, she could feel her heart thumping. There was a tang in the air she recognized as amniotic fluid. Obviously Sunset's water had broken, but how long ago she had no way of knowing. All she knew was that once strong contractions had started, and they obviously had, the foal should arrive in the next ten to twenty minutes.

If only I knew when they began!

139

She watched anxiously as Sunset struggled to give birth, fervently hoping the mare could finish the job without help.

The animal was sweating with effort, but Carole wasn't sure there was any progress being made. She squatted by Sunset's head, talking soothingly, but as the minutes ticked by she grew worried. She shifted her position to the rear so that she could look for the first signs of the foal's arrival.

She kept an eye on her watch. By her calculation the baby should be making its way into the world by now. Finally she spotted a cloudy white membrane emerging. She sighed with relief. Maybe everything was going to be all right after all.

Another contraction shook the mare and Carole could make out one tiny hoof and a little muzzle inside the birth sac. Her heart lurched. That wasn't right. Carole knew the foal should have *both* legs out in front, not just one.

Sunset was going to need help!

Abruptly the mare scrambled to her feet. This didn't alarm Carole because she knew it was common behavior at this stage of the birth. If there was a problem with the position of the foal inside the mother, standing up and lying down seemed to be nature's way of fixing things.

140

Unfortunately in this case there was no way for the horse to shift her foal enough to make a difference.

Carole felt panicky. Sunset was in pain, and if Carole didn't act fast both the baby and the mare could die! She knew what she needed to do, but without another person it looked almost impossible.

"Hey, C, what's going on?"

Carole whirled around, startled. Zach Simpson was standing behind her.

"Zach! What are you doing here? He started to answer but she cut him off. "Never mind, I'm just so glad you are I could hug you! We have to help Sunset! She's having her foal!"

Zach's eyes grew wide as he took in the situation. "Is that her baby coming out?"

"Yes, but something's wrong."

"Shouldn't she be lying down?"

"Yes and no," Carole told him impatiently. There was little time for explanations. If she was going to do this, she was going to have to do it soon or it would be too late. "I think one of the baby's legs is folded under. That means it will never fit through the birth canal."

Zach looked stricken. "Is it going to die?

"Not if I have anything to say about it," she told him determinedly.

141

"Do you want me to run to Pine Hollow and get help?"

Carole shook her head. "There's not enough time."

Zach looked as scared as Carole felt. "What can we do?"

"I'm going to try to pull its leg out from under it. But to do that I first have to push it back in."

Carole wouldn't have thought it possible but somehow Zach's eyes got even bigger and rounder. "No way! Are you telling me you're going to put your hands *inside* her?"

Carole nodded grimly. "At least one and most of my arm. The foal is still getting oxygen from the placenta, so it won't suffocate," she explained. "Now, I need you to keep Sunset as still as you can, okay?"

Zach nodded. "I'll try," he told her, taking the halter in his hands.

In spite of the mare's best efforts, the foal was still in the same position it had been a few minutes before.

Carole took a deep breath and, standing directly behind the horse, steeled herself for what she had to do. She waited only long enough for the last contraction to pass before placing her hands on the foal's foreleg and head. Her heart was beating a mile a minute. She was terrified of doing something wrong and injuring the little creature, but she knew that if she didn't try to help there'd be a dreadful price to pay. Slowly she began pushing it back inside its mother.

Sunset snorted and tried to move away but Zach held her firmly in place. Carole could hear him talking soothingly to her. *Good.* She figured the horse had a right to be at least as scared as the humans were.

Although there was resistance at first, once she had managed to push the baby out of the birth canal, it slid backward fairly easily.

"How's it going?" Zach called to her.

"So far so good," she told him. "This next part is the tricky bit. I have to find the leg and pull it free. That should put it back in the right position."

Carole pushed her arm into the birth canal as far as possible, feeling around the foal as best she could. Even though she knew approximately where the leg should be, it was still difficult to find without being able to see.

Agonizing moments passed as she searched. Everything felt slimy and bizarre. Finally she found what she thought was a knee. She struggled to get a firm grip on it but it was just out of reach of her hand.

Carole started to panic. She could barely reach the foal's knee, let alone get to its foot. If she didn't use her hand to cover the hoof, the baby could tear the uterine wall and that could kill Sunset!

Carole tried again. Her arm simply wasn't long enough! "Zach, I can't do it!" she cried.

"What are we going to do?" he asked anxiously.

Carole removed her wet arm as Sunset began to struggle.

"I think she wants to lie down again," Zach said.

Carole thought quickly. "Let her."

Zach did as he was told and the mare lowered herself back to the ground, grunting and groaning.

This was terrible. Carole's mind raced. She doubted the mare's lying down had made much difference in the position of the baby. Then it hit her. Zach was taller than she was and his arm was a couple of inches longer. Maybe he could do it.

"Zach, listen to me, you're going to have to try."

Zach looked incredulous. "Me? Are you crazy?" He shook his head. "I don't know anything about the insides of a horse. I barely know about the outsides."

"If you don't try they're going to die, both of them!" she told him urgently.

Sunset groaned in agony. The strain on her was tremendous. That seemed to make up Zach's mind.

"Okay, C," he said grimly. "You'll have to talk me through it."

Carole moved quickly. They were running out of time. "The baby has to have both front legs extended in front of it, like a diver. Right now one of them is bent under at the knee. You need to pull it straight."

Zach traded positions with her. "How do I do that? Just grab and pull?"

Carole placed a hand on the horse's head to comfort her. "Use your hand to cover the hoof. That will protect Sunset from internal injury. Then pull firmly and steadily."

Zach nodded and pushed his hand inside the mare. He looked terribly pale. Carole hoped he wasn't going to faint—she needed him too desperately.

Her position at the mare's head made it difficult for her to see what was going on. "How's it going?" she called anxiously.

"I think I've found the leg," he told her. "Just a little more . . . got it! I've got the foot!"

Carole's heart leaped. If he could only pull it straight, everything might be okay after all. She waited. And waited.

"Yes!" Zach finally cried.

"Yes?" she asked anxiously.

"They're both straight now." He stepped back, breathing hard.

Another spasm shook Sunset. Carole and Zach

held their breath, waiting for the outcome, knowing they had done all they possibly could for the poor creature.

Once again they watched as the baby struggled to find its way into the world. This time, however, it was different. Instead of getting stuck halfway, the foal slid smoothly and completely out of its mother.

"Look, it's a filly!" Carole said excitedly.

"C, why isn't it moving?" Zach asked.

A wave of fear washed over Carole. Zach was right. The baby wasn't stirring. She looked closer. There was no sign that it was even breathing. She felt tears coming to her eyes. "Oh, Zach, maybe we were too late," she whispered.

"C, we've got to do something!"

Carole shook her head helplessly. "I don't know what else to do."

The little foal showed no signs of life. It lay limply on the hard earth as if the struggle to be born had used up the tiny spark of life that had been in it.

Zach sank to his knees, reaching out and almost touching the unmoving filly. "It's not fair, he whispered. "She never even had a chance." A sob escaped him as tears started to flow.

Carole knelt down beside him, her own hot tears running down her cheeks unchecked. Her heart was breaking. "I'm to blame," she sobbed. "If I hadn't forgotten to lock that dumb door, if only I'd studied harder . . . Judy would have saved her. Oh, Zach, it's all my fault." She couldn't bear to look at the little creature before her. Its lifeless body was a searing accusation.

Zach slipped his hand into hers and she could feel him trembling. They were both too overcome with sorrow to speak.

Sunset looked down at her still baby and gave a little whinny. After sniffing it curiously for a moment, she nudged it with her nose and then began to lick it, removing the rest of the birth sac.

Suddenly the lifeless foal twitched and began to wiggle.

Carole stared, unable to believe her eyes. "Zach, it's breathing. It's alive!" she screamed joyfully.

"All right!" Zach hollered. "Yeehaw!"

The two of them hugged each other and jumped up and down.

The furry little newborn tolerated its mother's tender ministrations for a few minutes and then tried to get to its feet. The foal's struggle to stand on its impossibly long, spindly legs left Zach and Carole crying with laughter.

Sunset stood up and the little filly snorted at her

mother as if to say, *It's about time*. With wobbly little steps it moved over to the mare and began nursing.

Carole and Zach looked at each other. They were grubby, sweaty, covered with slime, and had tear tracks running down their faces—but they were glowing with happiness.

"C, do you remember when Stevie told me I hadn't lived until I'd washed under a horse's tail?"

"Sure."

He slipped an arm around Carole's shoulders as he watched Sunset and her new baby. "My friend, we sure are living large today."

13

AFTER THE NEWBORN finished nursing, she seemed overcome by sleepiness and awkwardly lowered herself to the ground for a nap. Sunset hovered over her baby protectively.

"I can't blame her for being tired," Carole said to Zach. "I'm a little beat myself."

"You could use a shower, too," he told her. "In fact, would you mind moving downwind from me?"

Carole punched him in the arm and laughed. "Have you looked in the mirror lately?"

Zach grinned. "I'll have to wash my hands before breakfast, that's for sure."

That reminded Carole just how early it was. "Hey,

what were you doing out here at this time of the morning, anyway?"

Zach looked sheepish. "I was using the shortcut to get to Pine Hollow. I needed to get my math book, and I figured no one would be around."

Carole was surprised to notice that they really weren't very far from Zach's backyard. She had been so intent on finding Sunset, she hadn't even realized where she was. "I guess it's a good thing for Sunset that you left your book there in the first place," she said solemnly. "You do know you saved their lives, don't you?"

Zach shook his head. "No way. If you hadn't been here, I wouldn't have had a clue about what to do."

"And I couldn't have done it by myself."

"I guess we could split the credit, then."

Carole grinned. "Not a chance. I'm taking all the glory on this one."

Zach laughed. "Hey! *Glory* would be a good name for the baby, don't you think?"

"Perfect," Carole agreed. "Too bad we don't get to name her. That's up to Mr. Wooten."

Zach shrugged. "Maybe he'll be open to suggestions. Anyway, it sure has been an exciting start to the day. I never dreamed I'd ever do something like that. The whole thing was awesome."

"If you enjoyed it so much, maybe you should consider becoming a veterinarian. I am."

Zach looked dubious. "Would I have to do something like that every day?"

"Maybe."

"Not a chance!" he told her emphatically. Then his eyes fell on the sleeping filly. "Well . . . it was pretty amazing."

"Even the part where you had to stick your hand inside?" Carole reminded him.

Zach nodded. "Yeah, C, even that part."

The little filly didn't nap for long, and once she was up on her stiltlike legs again, Carole decided it was time to make them walk back to Pine Hollow.

She led Sunset while Zach trailed behind with Starlight. She told him to keep the horse well back so that there'd be no danger of the foal getting stepped on or the mother being upset by the other animal's presence.

The return journey was uneventful, for which Carole was profoundly grateful. Since it was now almost eight o'clock in the morning, she knew everyone at Pine Hollow would be awake and no doubt worried about the missing mare.

Sure enough, when they came into view of the stable, Carole spotted Judy Barker's truck in the driveway.

She led the little group into the yard and was greeted by the veterinarian and an anxious Max.

"What on earth is going on?" Max demanded.

Carole felt herself blush with shame. "Sunset had her baby."

"So I noticed," he said, taking the mare's halter from her. "Is there some reason why she didn't have it in my stable as planned?" His eyes landed on Zach and Starlight. "And why were you out riding so early this morning?"

"Carole saved the foal's life," Zach told them excitedly.

Carole shook her head. "Actually, Zach saved both their lives. I'm the one who put them in danger in the first place."

Max frowned. "I don't understand. Judy said you called her from here last night."

"I did, but after I checked on Sunset, I guess I forgot to latch her stall door," she confessed. "I remembered it only this morning, so I came over to see if everything was all right, but she was gone. So I took Starlight to find her."

"First things first, Max," Judy said. "I need to know about the birth. You and Zach look like you had a rough time."

Carole smiled ruefully. She had forgotten what a mess they were. "I think Sunset had the worst of it. The foal had one of its legs tucked under, so it couldn't come out. I pushed it back in and tried to unfold its leg, but my arms weren't long enough. Luckily Zach has longer arms and he managed to do it."

Judy smiled broadly. "It sounds like you did everything right, Carole. I'm really proud of you." She looked over at the boy. "You too. That took a lot of courage, young man. Now with your permission, Max, I think I'd better take a look at mother and daughter."

Carole watched Judy lead the mare and foal away. She hung her head, unable to meet Max's eyes. "I'm so sorry, Max. I really blew it."

"Leaving the door unlatched was very careless," he agreed. "But thank goodness you had a careless moment."

Carole couldn't believe what she had just heard. She looked at Max in astonishment.

He put a hand on her shoulder. "Don't you realize that if you hadn't, you wouldn't have come back to check on her and Sunset might have died alone in her stall this morning?"

Carole hadn't thought of it like that. It made her

feel a little better. She had still messed up, but, strangely enough, it had turned out for the best.

Mrs. Reg appeared from inside the stable. "Carole, Lisa is on the phone. You can take the call in my office, but don't be long."

"Thanks, Mrs. Reg," Carole said, hurrying inside.

When she got to the phone she heard a worried Lisa hanging on the line. "What's going on? You sneak out of the house and leave us this note that says you have to go to Pine Hollow?"

"Calm down. Everything's fine. But you have missed out on some excitement. Sunset had her foal!"

Lisa's squeal of delight was so loud Carole was forced to move the phone away from her ear. "I don't believe it!" Lisa gasped with excitement.

Carole could hear Stevie in the background demanding to be let in on the news. When Lisa told her, Carole heard another shriek of joy.

Lisa came back on the phone. "I can't believe we missed it," she wailed.

"Actually you didn't miss it by much," Carole told her. "Anyway, I'll tell you all about it when you get down here."

"We're on our way," Lisa said and hung up.

Carole put down the phone and left the office. She

found Zach in Starlight's stall. He had untacked her horse and was giving him some water.

"Thanks, Zach," she said.

Mrs. Reg came down the hall toward them. "I heard you two had quite the adventure this morning, and I thought you could use a little pick-me-up." She handed them each a cup of hot chocolate.

"Thanks, Mrs. Reg. It smells great." Carole took the mug gratefully. There were even miniature marshmallows floating on the top, just the way she liked it.

"Sure does," Zach agreed. He took a tiny sip. "Yow! Be careful, C, it's pretty hot."

"I should hope so," Mrs. Reg sniffed. "I believe that is where the term *hot chocolate* came from. Why don't you two go sit down somewhere while you drink it. You both look a little worse for wear."

Carole led the way to the locker room and sank onto a bench.

Zach did the same. "Man, having babies sure is hard work."

Carole laughed. "You should try it from the other side sometime."

"Not something I'm ever going to have to worry about," Zach chuckled. "But, wow, that was something. Beats television hands down!"

Carole came to a decision. She had planned on waiting until Lisa and Stevie had arrived to talk to Zach, but this felt like the right moment. "Zach, did Mrs. Reg ever tell you about a pony named Sprinkles?"

He shook his head. "I don't think so."

She told him the story about the pony who was only good at walking. At the end the boy looked at her blankly. "I don't get it. What fun is just walking?"

"What's *fun* is doing something well," Carole replied. "Even if you can only do one thing, that's still better than not being able to do anything, right?"

"I guess," he said, taking a sip of his cocoa.

Carole put down her cup. "What I'm trying to say is, you love to ride fast and you love just being with your horse. That's what you do well. That's what makes you happy."

For the first time since the birth of the filly, Zach looked depressed. "That's never going to win me a blue ribbon."

"No, it's not. But, you know, Zach," she said as gently as she could, "some people don't like to compete in horse shows. It's simply not their thing. As a matter of fact, I've heard a theory that people who don't compete may have a better bond with their horse because their relationship is based purely on mutual pleasure. Neither the horse nor the rider is under any pressure."

Zach looked interested. "Not everyone who rides competes?"

"Of course not," she told him.

"But everyone around here does."

"We show our horses because that's fun for us. There may come a time when I won't want to do it anymore, and then I'll stop. But even if I do, I know I'll never give up horses."

"Are you saying I can just take classes and go for rides?" he asked cautiously. "I don't have to compete in the shows?"

Carole smiled. "Absolutely, and anyone who tries to tell you different is wrong. Someday you may decide to try it again, but until then Stevie and Lisa and I can show you lots of fun things to do on horseback."

Zach grinned. "Cool. I'll take you up on that, C." He looked at his watch. "Wow! I've got to go home." He leaped to his feet. "I kind of sneaked out without telling my folks. They're gonna be worried about me."

"In case you're interested, we're playing mounted games again next week."

"Count me in," he said enthusiastically.

Carole smiled. "See you in school tomorrow."

Zach headed for the door. He paused and turned to Carole. "Thank you," he said.

After he had left, Carole sat back to finish her hot chocolate. She was slurping the last few drops when Lisa and Stevie rushed in. "Hi, guys," she greeted them. "Have you seen the new foal yet?"

"We just came from her," Lisa gushed. "Have you ever seen anything so cute?"

"And funny," Stevie added. Then she stopped and stared. "Have you considered taking a shower lately?"

Carole laughed.

"You look terrible," Lisa informed her. "What have you been up to?"

"Didn't Max or Judy tell you?" Carole asked, surprised.

Stevie and Lisa shook their heads.

"I helped deliver Sunset's baby," she told them happily. "Actually, Zach and I did."

"Alone?" Stevie asked, clearly astonished.

"Yep! In the field."

Stevie and Lisa threw themselves down on the bench beside her.

"Okay, start talking," Lisa demanded. "And don't you dare leave out any of the details."

In the next few minutes Carole told them the entire

tale. Her two best friends were clearly amazed by the story.

"I can't believe a boy would do that," Stevie said. "Guess Zach isn't a typical boy after all."

"You must have been scared," Lisa said. "I know I would have been."

"I was," Carole admitted. But I was more scared for Sunset and her baby. Besides, we had no choice."

"You're really amazing, Carole," Stevie told her.

"You're going to make a fantastic veterinarian," Lisa added warmly.

"Do you suppose Judy goes through something like that every day?" Stevie wondered.

"Let's go find her and ask," Lisa suggested.

"Do you mind if we stop by Sunset's stall again first?" Carole pleaded. "I'd really like to take another look at her foal."

Stevie and Lisa didn't need coaxing. They were more than happy to take another peek at the baby.

A few moments later The Saddle Club was gathered outside the birthing stall, watching the pair. Nestled deep in the soft hay, the new little filly was sound asleep, and Sunset, who had been so restless for so long, was standing quietly and peacefully over her new baby.

"Judy said the filly's perfect," Carole whispered.

"She sure looks it from where I'm standing," Lisa said dreamily.

"You did an amazing thing today, Carole," Stevie said, putting a hand on her shoulder.

"Amazing," agreed Lisa.

Carole smiled dreamily. It had been amazing.

"Now," said Stevie, "about that shower . . ."

ABOUT THE AUTHOR

BONNIE BRYANT is the author of more than a hundred books about horses, including The Saddle Club series, The Saddle Club Super Editions, the Pony Tails series, and Pine Hollow, which follows the Saddle Club girls into their teens. She has also written novels and movie novelizations under her married name, B. B. Hiller.

Ms. Bryant began writing The Saddle Club in 1986. Although she had done some riding before that, she intensified her studies then and found herself learning right along with her characters Stevie, Carole, and Lisa. She claims that they are all much better riders than she is.

Ms. Bryant was born and raised in New York City. She still lives there, in Greenwich Village, with her two sons.